The Right Way

CROSSROADS TO FRESH STARTS

KELLY RAE

Contents

1. The Beginning — 1
2. Alone — 19
3. Unsure — 25
4. Uncovering — 33
5. Time Away — 36
6. A Meeting To Remember — 39
7. The Getaway Cabin — 44
8. Frazzled — 47
9. Traveling Home — 50
10. Thinkin' Problem — 53
11. Smothering Peace — 56
12. From A Distance — 59
13. Dying To Get Your Number — 62
14. Almost A Silent Night — 66
15. A Wake-Up Call — 69
16. Cooking With Emotions — 72
17. Drama — 77
18. Humbling — 82
19. To Call Or Not To Call — 84
20. Lost Without Her — 87
21. The Call — 90
22. Remembrance — 92
23. The Confession — 98
24. Coffee Shop Talk — 102
25. You Made Me Strong — 108
26. Innocent Feelings — 112
27. Coming Clean — 116
28. The Dreaded Phone Call — 121

29. Lynn's Reassurance   125

30. Getting Ready For A Trip   132

31. Just Lakin'   137

32. Brint's Love   141

33. Clint Remembers   144

34. Tanner Remembers   148

35. Letter Of Intent   156

36. Camping All Alone   159

37. Soul Search   163

38. Just Hangin'out With Andy   164

39. Feelings   168

40. Wine Time   171

41. Confiding In Andy   178

42. Clint's Camping Trip   182

43. Tanner's Confession   187

44. Girl Talk   190

45. Stay Positive   197

46. Hiccup At The Office   199

47. Sister Talk With A Chance Of Tears   202

48. Clint's Cuffing   209

49. Tanner's Prayer   212

50. Day Of Reckoning   215

51. Happily Ever After   217

About the Author   219

CHAPTER 1

The Beginning

Tanner sat at her mahogany desk, shuffling through the stack of papers that stretched from end to end. "Sara, can you bring me the Copeland file? Oh! Bring a refill for my coffee, I'm going to need it!" Sounding a bit uptight as opposed to her usual jovial self, Sara was genuinely concerned. Tanner had been burning the midnight oil, working on the Copeland land project that was going to court in a couple of weeks. She was accustomed to these high-profile cases, but this one in particular had her exhausting herself. Opposing Clint, Clinton G. Winstead, the most sought-after attorney in Chicago, meant she needed to bring her A game from start to finish. The other reason she quickly pushed from her mind was nausea which comes and goes. She looked up at her diploma from Vanderbilt University elongating her neck, the touch of her mother's tender fingers on her shoulders, she told herself, not this time! Turning to her computer she began researching to find an article of interest. She reclined back in her black leather chair, and holding her coffee mug with both hands, she took in a deep breath filling her lungs with the smell of coffee which warmed her from head to toe. She continued reading and before she knew it, the clock strummed seven o'clock. Pushing her hands away from her desk, she stood. She looked down at her desk and the stacks of papers, telling herself, "There is just so much you can do in a day." She twisted to look out her 17th floor window. A late-night rain had begun and with it the memories came flooding back again. She stared at the raindrops trickling down the windowpane and as she stood there in the silence, she felt tears begin to dampen her cheeks. Gently touching the cold window with her fingertip, tracing the pattern of the rolling rain drops, she stared out across the loop. Forcing away her pain once more, she tucked her feelings away, pushing them down even deeper. It was like tucking a handkerchief in her shirt pocket. She pulled her shoulders back once more and turned to gather her things.

On the drive home she searched through station after station before finally turning off the radio. She linked her phone certain she would find a favorite, but nothing appeared to satisfy her mood tonight. Thinking to herself, "Geez! Why? Why today? Why now?," as she turned down the last stretch of road leading home. All she thought about was how far away she could get. Completely lost in her thoughts, she found herself parked in her usual spot. Slightly switching off her car she sat staring into the night. It was black and the rain rolled down her window. She gazed at the drops changing colors as they caught the different colored lights of her surroundings. Today had drained her.

Tanner walked through her front door, threw her keys on the hutch, and flipped on the tiny light that used to be her grandmother's. It always greeted her with such warmth in her childhood when she would visit her grandma and now it still made her heart yearn for the love and warm feelings only a grandma could provide. Tonight, was no different. The drive home in the mid-September rain did nothing more than add to the stress of her day. All she thought about was the sensation of warm water flowing over her physically exhausted body.

She didn't waste any time getting undressed when she got home. Slowly tipping her head under the water faucet, closing her eyes, she ran her hands through her silky brown hair, finding her shoulders and giving herself a slight squeeze. As the water enveloped her body, the thoughts came flowing back as well. She shook her head as if trying to shake herself to reality. It was real and painful and suffocating. She reached for the soap trying her best to carry on with reality. She finished washing off the day and forced herself to get out of the bathtub. She had searched for her perfect claw foot tub for months, when she saw an estate sale in Savannah, Georgia. She knew she would need it, specifically for days like today.

Noticing her tiny white toenails, Tanner thought to herself, "You have to take better care of yourself!" She wrapped herself tightly in her thick, terry robe. It was safe and comforting. It was the dull, creamy, pink color of the towel which relaxed her she searched for this serenity on a regular basis. Although, it seemed nothing helped her find peace tonight. She wandered to the kitchen, flipped on the light, and fixed herself some tea. The aroma of chamomile filled her senses and brought back a bit of much-needed clarity. As she took another sip from her favorite mug, she could feel the warmth run down the inside of her body.

Wondering to her living room, her cat Berkeley headed towards their favorite chair. Berk loved to snuggle in the fluffy, white pillows with Tanner. Each of them found their comfy position and began staring into the perfect flames of the tiny, gas fireplace. With a vengeance, the thoughts came rushing back to her yet again! Pushing them away once more, she embraced her fluff ball asking herself, "Why today, why tonight?"

As she lifted her mug to her lips, the phone rang. After looking at the caller ID, she answered in the most cheerful voice she could find. "Hey mom, what's up?" Tanner said trying to be cheery. Her mom always knew when she was pushing her best self forward! She also realized she did it for her sake. Madeline loved her daughter dearly. She wanted all the happiness and success in the world for her. She had encouraged her daughter to follow her heart to live and embrace every day to its fullest. "Make decisions with the end in mind and no regrets," her mom would often remind her.

Tanner was the most serious of her two daughters, she worked hard to keep her as lighthearted as possible. This would be a difficult task she would face on a daily basis. "Hi, sweetheart, you're just getting in, aren't you?" Her mother understood Tanner burned the midnight oil more often than not, and it concerned her. "Yeah, well you know I go to court in a week on the Copeland case, and I don't think there are enough hours in a day to make me feel fully prepared this time. I am actually in a bit early tonight," she responded to her mother.

Tanner enjoyed her career of choice and could not imagine doing anything else. She loved to help the underdog. It was a passion of hers, because, growing up, she always felt that she was one. It began when one of her teachers told her she had 'cheerleader' written all over her. The condescending remark stuck in the back of her head for years, pushing her to prove there was depth to her and she had what it took to be a real asset to society: that is when she began pulling for the underdog.

This time the client wasn't the underdog, it was her. Tanner didn't want to face Clint Winstead in court. It was something she had feared would happen one day, and now it was here. C. W. was known for not playing fair. He was harsh, manipulative, and stopped at nothing to win. Her mother knew her daughter and knew she would physically and mentally work herself to death to guarantee she gave this case, as she did with every case, all she had. "Honey, I know that you are not getting enough rest, and I know that you are probably not eating like you should. Are you eating well?" Madeline asked. "I am fine," Tanner responded trying not to get irritated. "Yes, but you need to keep up your health right now, you know what happens when you don't take care of yourself."

Her mom always saw her in a more fragile state than she saw herself. Tanner reminded herself daily she was the picture of health. She was happy for the most part and received good reports each year from her physical. "Mom, stop it! I am fine. What is Lex up to this week? Did she get settled in to school all right? I haven't had time to call and check in like usual, with this case, about the wedding. She is coming in next week for the fitting, right?" asked Tanner, changing the subject to a more lighthearted topic.

She knew if she didn't, the conversation may turn tense, and she hated edgy conversations with her mom. She knew her mom loved her and her sister so much that sometimes she could feel the pain only such a strong love could feel. "Yes, as far as I know. You know your sister, she changes her mind, hair, clothes, whatever with the slightest change of the wind," Madeline said. Tanner and Alexa weren't only sisters, they're best of friends. Sometimes Tanner thought Alexa took advantage of her love and friendship. Alexa was a carefree spirit. She floated through life as if she was on her very own cloud making its way across the universe. She picked up on a whim and went where she pleased. If it was an idea, it would come to pass for her. From the outside, it seemed as if everything her sister touched turned to gold. She flew by the seat of her pants, and nothing ever worried her or get under her skin.

Deep down, Tanner held a bit of resentment toward her for this. She, being the firstborn, had all eyes on her. However, when Alexa came along, her parents figured out life didn't have to look perfect. They allowed her little sister to slide through life without the expected perfection her parents had instilled in her at such a young age. Alexa could make mistakes; Tanner's bar was set to a higher level of accountability. Such a life had lent itself to the pressure Tanner put on herself to then reflect her upbringing, and that she worked her fingers to the bone to keep it up.

"Well, if you speak to her, tell her I love her and I can't wait to see her," said Tanner. "Lex would not miss this last fitting for the world, no matter what came up. She is excited for you," her mom said. "I know, it's just things are moving so fast lately, and we haven't had time to keep up with one another like we normally do.

It feels like we are drifting apart," replied Tanner. "You and Lex will never drift, you two are way too in tune with one another without any wiggle room. You two always had one another's back, and I've always been the last to find out anything," Mom explained. "I know, I just have a lot on me, mom. With that, I really need to go. I haven't had a chance to talk to Brint all week. He had to leave again unexpectedly," Tanner sighed. "Why do you sound so, I don't know, sarcastic when you say that? You know he is just as dedicated to his career as you are darling. You have known this for two years," her mom reminded her. "Mom, I have to go, you know I love you and I'll talk to you tomorrow," Tanner said to end the call. "To the moon and back sweet pea," her mother said her goodbyes. "Night mom," Tanner said, and, with that, she hung up. She knew she should pick up the phone right then and call Lex, but she just didn't have the energy. She sunk deeper into her chair and fell sound asleep.

Awaking to the sound of her fiancé's voice was always a pleasant surprise. Brint's job called him away unexpectedly from time to time, and when it did, there was little time for talk and goodbyes. He leaned down and brushed Tanner's hair from her eyes. Shifting in the chair, she sensed Brint's presence and slowly sat up. "Hey, sweet lady," he spoke softly.

She rose to her feet without thought, finding her balance, he helped steady her placing his strong hands on her shoulders. Reaching for her face with one hand, pulling her closer with the other hand, he leaned down to kiss her forehead, moving down to her cheek, pecking it ever so gently and then to her lips. There's a feeling of safety and security when she was in his arms. His scent was just as comforting. She took in a deep breath, and she felt the calmness it created for her. This was something special. She would know him with her eyes closed in a line up. This was a characteristic she looked for in a mate. There had only been one other, so long ago, that could calm her as Brint did. This was how she knew without a doubt he was the one she would lay with every night. She would wake to him in the morning light each day and never want for anything for the rest of her life.

He had already undressed from his day. Leading her to their bedroom, they snuggled into bed, pulling the pale, blue comforter around them. He wrapped his arm around her and gently pulled her to him. She could feel the stress of her day melt away as their bodies conformed to one another. Again, she took a deep breath, sighed a little sigh of complete and utter happiness, and they both fell fast asleep.

The buzzing of the alarm clock had Tanner's heart racing. Looking toward the bathroom, she heard the shower and could smell the faint scent of lavender and white musk. It was fresh and masculine. It fit Brint's image to a tee. He was a genuine man, he made friends wherever he went, and people seemed to gravitate toward him. He had a firm handshake and smiling eyes. He was a specimen of genetic perfection, and he didn't have to work for it. This characteristic made Tanner a bit jealous. She admired his ability to abstain from unhealthy tendencies. He took good care of himself naturally.

She made her way to the kitchen to put on a pot of coffee and turn on the TV to catch up on the local news. Returning from the kitchen, she met Brint in the steamy bathroom. She hopped up on the counter to get his attention. Catching a glimpse of wanting in her eyes he turned to her, placing his hands on her thighs and a kiss on her forehead, "Good morning sweet lady," Brint greeted her. "Good morning, I have your coffee brewing," she said. "Super!" he replied bluntly. "Something on your mind? You left so suddenly the other morning and got home so late. Anything you want to talk about?" Tanner inquired. "You know I would if I were able. I just have a situation that I am dealing with at the office," he said to remind her of his confidentiality.

Brint worked for the State Attorney's office and took his job very seriously. He was so dedicated that he almost forgot to breath. Thank goodness for the involuntary action. Trying not to sound whiny, she asked. "Will you be home tonight? I really need some time with you. The final touches are being put on the wedding and you know I have been working the Copeland case. There are so many things begging for my attention, and I want you and your attention!"

"AHH, you want me that's a provoking thought," he inquisitively inquired. "Come on, you know what I mean," she replied. "I do," he answered. "Sweet, we will have plenty of time to soak up each other on the honeymoon," he grinned. "Speaking of our honeymoon, where are we going?" she asked. "You know it's a secret, you'll know when we get there. I promise that I will not disappoint you and thought of everything. Your every need will be met!" he assured her. "Why does everything have to be so secretive with you?" she argued. "It keeps you on your toes and I like watching you try to figure it out," he laughed.

"It will be my life's pleasure, I'm sure. Well, I am glad I gave you a kick. So, before I give you another kick, you better let me get in the shower. I will see you tonight," she said as she smiled and leaned to kiss him on his cheek.

The tone, the one that told Brint he's pushing his limits with her were present and accounted for. "Yes, sweet angel, I will do my best." With that, she bounced off the counter and disappeared into the steam. Looking at her silhouette, he saved the image and knew he better return promptly. Later that day, Tanner finished the outline of her opening statement and felt pleased with what was to come in the upcoming weeks. She would be facing her long-awaited nemesis; Clinton Winstead and his father, Greer.

They were a force to be reckoned with.

Greer had gone up against Tanner's father on many occasions throughout their dueling careers and now it was her turn to face his son in court. While her father, Spencer Bingham, had a very respectable career in the Illinois court system, his one defeat was not beating Greer. They had graduated from the University of Chicago law and ended up practicing in the same judicial system. Greer always made negative innuendo references toward Spencer's Southern upbringing, but he never let this bother him. He was confident in himself. However, over the years, Tanner let it fester under her skin. When she and Clinton would attend a party of a mutual friend growing up, he would mock her father's Southern manners, her mother's gentle characteristics, and her own Southern drawl. Alexa was too young to remember or care. Tanner felt as though she would fight this fight for the rest of her life.

Pausing to remember one spring picnic that was held annually, a shiver came over her body. Home on spring break, she was urged to join her parents at the annual Spring to Life fundraiser. This was an event her parents were huge sponsors of along with the majority of whose the who's in town. Tanner hated these events but always loved talking with her mother about everything she had overheard throughout the day's events and comparing stories. A few years ago, while putting together delightful bouquets of fresh flowers for the men to buy their ladies, Clint strolled up to her table way too confidently for her liking. He flipped out a crisp, one- hundred-dollar bill, "I would like a bouquet of pink tulips with baby's breath, please," he said. Handing Clint, the bundle, she politely said, "Thank you," as she placed the money in the bin. Clint turned to walk away and quickly did a 360 and held out the flowers, "For you."

Reluctantly reaching for the flowers, Tanner replied, "Thank you? For what have I done to deserve these?" she asked. Not sure if it was a genuine gesture or not, she waited for the tone in his reply to guide her. Clint said, "Um, I'm sorry," he said in a low tone. Standing there completely stunned by the words she had just heard. She smelled the flowers and admired their beauty. Turning away, Clint looked down at the ground and began to walk away. "Wait! Clint! Thank you, the flowers are nice," Tanner said genuinely and praying that she would not regret it later.

Later that day, after a very successful fundraiser, Tanner was kissing her father and mother goodbye when Clint walked up to her side. Spencer gave him a chiding look. "Dad, we're OK, really," she explained. Spencer did not approve of either of his girls taking up with a Winstead. Madeline never wasted any time filling her husband in on the earlier exchange of pleasantries. Giving her mom and dad a smile, Tanner turned toward Clint, took a step toward the fountain, "Shall we?"

Tanner was confident in the woman she had become and was continuing to develop into. She was steadfast in her meaning in this world and the mark she was certain to make on it. She always remembered her grandmother telling her, "One day, young lady you will head out into this great big world, and you must be deliberate. Life does not happen to you, but you will happen to your life. Do you understand me?" she commanded.

Tanner had the ultimate respect for her grandmother and would live every day to make good on her promise. Today, would be no different. Walking to the fountain, finding a nearby bench, Tanner sat quietly looking at the sunset over Lake Michigan. Contemplating why, after all the years of mockery, Clint was being such a gentleman. After a couple of minutes of small talk, they realized there was not much to catch up on. It's not like they had a past to speak about, Tanner decided to cut to the chase. "Clint, why today? Why now?" she asked. Showing a glimpse of the 'old' Clint, "Why not?" he replied. Leaning in to kiss her cheek, Tanner abruptly backed away. "Clint! What are you doing?" "I spend the majority of my childhood being made fun of by you and your brothers, then you buy me some flowers and you think you have permission to kiss me. No! Just No!" she yelled in disbelief. "Tanner, don't you understand all those years of making fun of you; I was trying to let you know I liked you! I have always had a place for you from the time we were like five years old, but you pushed me out of your way, just over there," pleading and pointing in the direction of the monkey bars. "You looked at me and told me I couldn't catch you! I feel like I've been working up the courage to catch you since that day," sighed Clint after confessing his feelings for Tanner.

Taken aback for a moment, Tanner gathered her thoughts before responding, "Well, you certainly had a funny way of showing it," she said sarcastically. "Listen, I am sorry for not letting you in on my agenda, but we are older now and I thought that it was time to get in line," said Clint. "In line?" she asked. "To have a chance to spend time with The Tanner Bingham, future attorney at law?" he explained. "Wow, you just hit the fast- forward button," she laughed.

Bringing herself back to the present, she closed her files for the day. With a deep sigh she straightened her desk and gathered her things. She stopped at her office window, as she did each day, to take in the scenery. Recently, it was the same. She felt that pang inside of her that left her feeling a bit empty, a bit melancholy, and it took her to a distant place. It was deep.

Although, she did not know the name of this place, it was real. She felt it with every inch of her being. Watching the sunset, she pictured herself floating on water, bobbing aimlessly in a paper mâchè boat, being drowned slowly until she was gone. Pulling herself away from this place once more, she flipped off her light and stopped at Sara's desk.

Sara was a constant in her life these days. She was in charge of keeping her on schedule. Sara also decided which calls made it through and which ones ended up on a sticky note on her desk. Tanner liked sticky notes as opposed to an emailed message. She could touch them and deal with them and it made her feel accomplished as they disappeared.

Sara kept Tanner's well-being in check by making sure she was fed and hydrated. She was the prime component in helping her succeed. They were a great team and had grown to become great friends. Sara took one look at Tanner and could see the anxiety building. There was a part of her that could feel it too. "Tanner, I am going to mark off some time tomorrow for you to take care of you. You have been working so hard these past few weeks. You have a lot going on in the upcoming weeks with last minute wedding details and the Copland Case. You just need some "you" time off," Sara explained.

Tanner threw her head back and laughed. "Oh Sara, have you been talking with my mom again?" she asked. "No, not today, Do I need to give her a call?" Sara replied. "NO! If nothing is brewing, for goodness's sake, let's not start something. I am good, I just really have a lot on my mind, and I am focusing on taking things one day at a time. Isn't that what you tell me to do?" she said. "Yes, you have to take care of you, too. Promise?" Sara asked. "Promise!" "Oh, Brint called about an hour ago and said that he was running late, but he would be home," she added. "Yeah, I kind of put an ultimatum of sorts on him this morning. I'm glad it seems he took me seriously," said Tanner.

"Well, no joke, I am marking an hour out of your day tomorrow, you can do what you want with it, but you are leaving this office and doing something," Sara demanded. "Ok, fine." Tanner headed toward the elevator looking back toward Sara's desk where she had returned to her computer.

She yelled, "Sara, thanks!" Without looking up, Sara replied "You got it!"

Turning the ignition switch to her white Mercedes GLC, she paused, placed her hands on the wheel, dropped her head slowly, and began to cry. Pangs in her chest returned, and she felt like she was suffocating again. This feeling was popping up at random times with no rhyme. Oh, there was a reason, but she flat out refused to acknowledge what was going on. Shaking her head, trying to shake the feeling that enveloped her, she turned on the radio. This was a place where she found herself drowning out her thoughts. Every night she would anxiously, almost frantically, search through her radio stations, or the music on her phone, looking for that one song that would take her away from the reality closing in on her.

Instead of going home, she found herself at the Lakefront Trail. Switching off the ignition, she sat in silence for a couple of minutes, which seemed like an hour, staring into the darkness, and listening to the silence. Silence. It had a sound, a rhythm. It wasn't the same as white noise, it was deeper and mysterious. The distant sound of a siren broke the silence, and she pushed open her car door.

Familiar with her surroundings, but very aware of the danger that could lurk in such a beautiful place at night, made her senses on edge. She found her way to a park bench just off the shoreline, where she sat down. Looking into the distance and feeling the wind off of the lake, she leaned back and filled her lungs with the precious gift of air. Slowly releasing it, she relaxed her shoulders and pulled out her phone. She sent Brint a text message, "Hey hon, it's my turn to do a disappearing act for a bit, I will be home after a while." Intentionally vague, she thought it may spike his blood pressure a bit, but what the heck.

As the wind whipped through her hair, she searched for peace. Now, she was focused and ready to face her thoughts, her feelings from deep down once and for all. Trying to wrench them from the depths of her soul, she found herself struggling. She buried her head in the palms of her hands and began to weep. Suddenly, she felt it. There it was like a thick smoke, smothering her. Like two hands, slowly massaging her heart, squeezing ever so slightly, just enough to cause a too familiar pain, she screamed into the darkness at the top of her lungs. "You hurt me! I Ioved you with all that I had, and you gave me nothing in return!" Sobbing, she looked up at the stars and continued. Talking aloud to herself now, instead of the world, she yelled, "You were all I knew, you were all I needed, you filled me up with happiness, you made me feel alive, you taught me to think for myself and to face my challenges. You helped me find me, only to leave me not knowing who I was anymore and taking my heart with you. You never even asked for it!" Tanner cried. She took a deep breath and found her foundation again.

She bowed her head in prayer, "Dear God, my Father in Heaven. You have heard my voice; you have felt my pain. You have seen me through my fears. You showed me that I should feel thankful for these feelings of love and feelings of despair. You have shown me how strong I, AM, on my own with you. You have shown me the path to real happiness the kind I find within myself. You have shown me that all I need is YOU. Dear Lord, I am so thankful for the broken roads that have led me to where I am this very moment. At this time, I ask that you give me clarity about the life ahead of me. I find myself before You once more, begging for direction. I am prepared to listen, please just show me the way, Your way. I ask for these things in Your name, AMEN."

Lowering her head and finding her way to her feet, she stood slowly. Looking toward the vast darkness, she started sifting through her thoughts one by one. After exhausting herself in her emotions, she sighed and found some relief, but for how long.

Returning to her car, she turned the key and heard her cell phone come to life. Brint was calling. She had been so caught up in her moment, that she didn't realize he had left three messages. "Hello! Sweet, Are you all, right? You have me terribly worried. What could have you wanting to disappear and what kind of jab is that anyway?" Brint asked.

Backing off, he realized this may not be the moment to press her, he stopped. "Listen, I know you have a lot on you, if you need time, I am home, I will be here when you get here. Take your time. I just have to know if you are, OK?" he said. Sounding a bit shaken and out of breath from the energy she had just spent, she responded. "Yes, I'm fine. I have had a lot on me, and today was not an easy one. I just needed some fresh air. I am on my way." "OK, are you sure you're all, right?" Brint asked again. "Yes, I promise, I'm fine," she reassured him.

As she walked through the front door, she was greeted by Berkeley and Brint. She felt safe. The kind of safe that let her know that she was where she needed to be. She wrapped her arms around Brint and raised to her tiptoes to place a gentle kiss on his cheek. Picking her up, he carried her to the living room where he had soft music playing, her favorite blanket draped across the arm of the couch and a bottle of wine chilling with two glasses. He also had her favorite pjs laid out.

Lowering her to the couch, he gently grasped the bottom of her sweater and pulled it over her head, making sure not to snag her earrings. He looked deep into her eyes. He reached for her night shirt and gently pulled it over her head. He swept her hair away from her eye and tucked it ever so carefully behind her ear. Leaning into her, he whispered, "I love you, and I am here for you."

Delicately placing a kiss on her cheek, he sat down beside her. She pulled her knees toward her, placed her head on his chest, and, with the flickering of the fire and the familiar thump of his heart, she fell fast asleep. Brushing her brow and leaning his head atop hers, he could smell the sweet fragrance of her shampoo, the faint smell of laundry detergent, and the crisp scent of the outdoors. Loosing himself in her sweetness, he drifted off to sleep himself.

CHAPTER 2

Alone

The air was crisp. The heat from the September sun had faded along with the chaos of the day. The breeze from Lake Michigan made its way through Clint's hair like the fingers of a stranger trying to seduce him for the first time. His thoughts were deep and concentrated.

Taking a sip from his high ball, letting the whiskey seep into his mouth, closing his eyes, he tried to imagine the kiss that made him numb all over and find the tingle on the back of his neck. Reality told him that it was just him and Johnnie Walker Platinum Label (Clint only drank the very best). Looking at his half empty glass, "Well Johnnie, it's just you and me old buddy."

Resting his glass on the arm of his lounge chair, he picked up the phone to dial for takeout. In the city, they delivered until midnight. He was thankful for this service and didn't mind the price. He hated to cook for himself although it was one of his favorite past times. He saw all hours of the night, as it was difficult for him to sleep these days.

Lost in thought, he was startled when the phone rang. "Mr. Winstead, your order from Dale's Bistro is here." "Yes, send them up." Dale's Bistro and Bar was a local favorite. Everything on the menu was a family secret recipe. The meat was aged to perfection. Usually, he would stop by after work, but tonight he was exhausted from the day and had the need to be alone with his thoughts. The doorbell rang and he hurried to the door. "Good evening, Clint, we missed you tonight, long day?" the bartender asked him. "You bet! I have a big case I have been working on. I may be by tomorrow night," replied Clint. "We will be there. We love your company," Jeff commented. "Yeah man, you too, later," he said. Clint had become great friends with the owner's son, who was an aspiring chef and was one of the best bartenders around. Jeff was friendly with everyone. He was the kind of bartender that made everyone welcome to stay as long as they liked. He remembered everyone's favorites and had them ready as soon as he saw them hit the door. Jeff would one day inherit this masterpiece of a bar from his father. He and his sister Gwen would keep the thirty-year family tradition moving forward.

After fixing a place at the end of the glass, dining room table (with seating for ten, he looked to his left and felt a void that could not be described. He hated eating alone. He longed to share his day with someone that cared about it, someone who had and an investment in him and his accomplishments. Clint wanted to wake up in the morning and have a meaning to his day. He wanted someone to love and take care of, a higher responsibility than just himself. However, no one had crossed his path that had met his standards. There were many, but by the fifth month, he would say goodbye, good luck, and he would be alone again.

He had felt love and the happiness that it brings. It made his days feel effortless. It put a skip in his step, and what felt like and extra beat in his heart that even made his head feel light. His world seemed more exact. Even the colors were more vibrant than he had ever remembered them being. However, as today came to an end, everything was just normal.

He put his plate in the sink. Jillian, his housekeeper would wash it in the morning. He shut the french doors to his balcony and turned the lock, then made his way through the apartment turning off the lights and disappeared into the shower. With the heat of the water running over him, he felt somewhat relaxed. He never lingered long. He switched off the water and grabbed the white towel he had draped over the shower door and wrapped it around his waist.

Wiping the steam from the mirror, he found his reflection. He brushed his thick, brown hair, tweaking some random grays that were starting to appear. Thinking to himself, to cover or not to cover. Nah, they say women like it. It is a sign of wisdom. But am I wise? He finished brushing his teeth and putting on a spritz of deodorant, he put on his night pants and retreated to bed. He opened his bedroom window slightly to let in the sounds of the city. He hated falling asleep in silence. He switched on the television to catch the nightly news, finding nothing on, but the latest crime stories, he turned the television off. Tucking his pillow and nuzzling in the white sheets, quickly fell asleep.

He could feel the warmth of her beside him. He rolled over and pulled her to him, their bodies like a hand in a glove, now intertwined, awakening slowly. His nose brushing against the nape of her neck, he began kissing her, feeling her respond. He wrapped his arm over her, cuddling her sweetly. He knew every curve in the darkness.

Abruptly sitting up in bed, sweat dripping down his brow, he looked at the pillow beside him and feels a stabbing in his heart. It was just a dream.

Making his way to the kitchen for a cold glass of water he begins to awaken a bit more. He brings himself back to reality. After a couple of sips, he headed back to the bedroom. Standing in front of the window, feeling the slight breeze embrace his body, he knew that he must force himself back to the bed.

Lying there in the darkness, he could hear his own heart beating. It is fast and his breathing is labored. He feels like the weight of an elephant is sitting on him. He just can't shake the memories that take him back to a time when he was so alive. There was something about her. The chemistry between them had never been duplicated. Every time they were within inches of each other it seemed their lips would find one another. Their bodies eventually catching up, and it would last for hours. Pure insanity, he thought. Like a moth to a flame, just as their relationship. Tossing the other direction, grasping the covers in his right hand, and pulling them under his arm as if embracing her once more, he closed his eyes.

He awakened once more, this time by a buzzing alarm clock. He pounded the tiny button as if it were a bug that was going to kill him, and he sat up. Catching a glimpse of his latest dream, his heart skipped a beat making his blood pressure rise and his pulse race. As he stood, he felt breathless and dizzy. Shaking his head, he pushes the memory from his mind and headed to the shower. Turning to the mirror, he sees his hair is everywhere and says to himself, "Damn, C! You look like hell! Just call her, get this over with." Hearing the voice of reason, "You can't just do that after all these years. You were the one that left. You were the one that walked away and treated her with the utmost disrespect. You my friend are an idiot." Out loud, Clint responds, "I AM, NOT!" Shaking his head, completely baffled that he has just answered himself, he steps into the steaming glass enclosed shower. Looking down at the tiny white, rectangular tiles, watching the water drain down the tiny holes in the floor, he is lost again.

As the speakers come to life, so does he. The rain is beating against the windows and the thunder is threatening. Through the flashing light from the lightning just outside of the window, he can see the silhouette of her small frame. Facing one another, they start to sway to the beat of "Fade into You," by Mazzy Star. Lowering her to the aged quilts placed on the floor, they became familiarly entangled!

Jolted back to reality once more by the sting of the hot water, he springs back to life. Shaking his head, and thinking "What the hell is wrong with me?" Feeling spent from his recent recollection, he cools the water and is finally ready to face the day. Approaching his black Mercedes AMG GT- Coupe, he begins to whistle. He sees his reflection in the paint thinking to himself. "Today is the day." Making a sharp right turn from the parking garage, "This Hearts on Fire," by Wolf Parade exploding through the speakers, aloud this time, he says "Yes, today is the day!"

CHAPTER 3

Unsure

Brint was finding it difficult to concentrate. He could not stop staring out of the window and watching the wind move the multiple shades of green. Startling him from his mesmerized state," Hey! Would you like to grab some lunch?" "Sure, let me grab my jacket." "So, what did you think about the Merliano Bust? 57 arrests not bad." "Yeah, that was great! Noah must be flying high today." "He sure is, seven years in the making, he's not coming down anytime soon! You feel like Tony's Place or Mr. Sub?" "Ah, I don't know, I'm not that hungry, I just needed some fresh air."

Like the two of them were on auto pilot, they stepped into Mr. Sub without further discussion. Upon finding two seats at the counter, Andy yells, "Two, Italian's all the way!" Picking up where Brint left off, "Not hungry, fresh air, what the hell man! In nine years, I have never known you to not be hungry, and I have never known you to need fresh air, seriously? With the hours you log in front of your computer, I thought Tanner might be trying to figure out a way to have the wedding in your office or at least the rehearsal dinner!"

"Ha, ha, you're too funny." "Then what's up? Talk to an old guy." "I don't think taking advice from a three timer is such a good idea!" "They say third time is a charm! Two years and going strong!" "They haven't started passing out awards yet!" "TOUCHÉ!"

"Am I doing the right thing? I mean we are crazy about each other! We have seen each other through happy times, sad times. When her grandmother passed, that really shook her up. They talked every day. We grew so close, and now, two years later and approaching our wedding day, I have never felt so distant from her." "What, this is, is a classic case of cold feet, get over it!" "No, this is colder than cold feet, this feels like Alaska, and I forgot my shoes!" "I'm going to give you some of your own medicine, talk to her! Yeah, I know, sounds simple. This is the woman that you are going to be spending the rest of your life with. If you don't learn to talk things out now, you are in for a long, hard life together and believe me, divorce is horrible," "I know. I need to. I am leaving work at five as I should, and I am going to talk to her." Just then, the sandwiches arrived, and simultaneously their phones rang. "Can we have these to go?"

Brint looked at the clock, 4:50 p.m. He thought he better give Tanner a call before heading home and expecting her too just be there. They both had such unpredictable schedules. "Hey sweet, it's B, call me when you get this love you." Before he could hit the glowing red button, it turned green. It was Tanner returning his call. "B, what's up?" "Hey, any plans after work, or are you working late?" "Um no, I don't have anything tonight. I was kind of thinking that, after last night, I needed some time at home with you. I was actually going to text you to see if you were going to be running late, but when you called, I thought it may be an emergency." "Well, yes, it is urgent, but not an emergency." "Is anything wrong?" "No, no, I'll see you tonight then. I will pick up Chinese, so don't cook anything."

Hearing an urgency in Brint's voice, she felt a notion of concern in her stomach. The kind that hits you right at the base of your sternum and causes you to have labored breathing yourself. All sorts of thoughts were running through Tanner's mind. Has he been called away again on some assignment to begin as soon as they return from their honeymoon, is he in some kind of danger? Oh, God! No, he doesn't want to get

Stopping herself, "Geez, I sound like my mom." She said in a whisper, grabbing her keys and purse, she fled her office as if there were a five- alarm fire, yelling, "I'm gone for the day, see you tomorrow!" With that, she disappeared.

As she walked through the door, she flipped on her grandmother's light, threw her keys in the basket beside it and headed to the bedroom to change. As she emerged from the bedroom in what Brint always called his favorite warn out blue jeans and white v-neck tee, she made her way to the kitchen to pour herself a glass of wine. She chose her favorite one. Brint always told her that it wasn't wine. To her, it came in a wine bottle, was made by a wine company, and had a cork. It was wine. He said it was too sweet to be wine. However, that is the way she liked it, and when it came to this, his opinion didn't matter. If he didn't want to drink it, he didn't have to. Standing at the counter, she took a sip, followed by a deep breath. She pulled her shoulders back and relaxed her stance.

Just then, she heard the dead bolt turn, the door unlocks, and Brint entered the house. Standing in the doorway with his deep brown hair in a bit of disarray, his top button of his crisp, white dress shirt already unbuttoned, and his tie already untied, she couldn't keep her mind from wondering. He threw his keys in the basket. "B, you really are home early!" Placing the food on the counter, he kissed her forehead softly and said, "I am going to go get comfortable."

She stood at the island and continued to sip her wine. When Brint came up beside her, she could feel the warmth of his body and smell the faint scent of his cologne. It was a smell that made her warm inside from head to toe. She did her best to refocus as she turned to get two plates from the cabinet and the silverware from the drawer. "Couch or dining room?" Brint asked. "Um, let's eat in the dining room." Tanner put their plates in their usual places without giving it a second thought. They sat in silence as they filled their plates. Without fail, they took a bite of their food simultaneously, then placing their forks on their plates they looked up at each other. They both began to speak, interrupting each other, they both stopped. Tanner said quickly, "I'm sorry, you go first." "You were the one that called to see if I was going to be home."

Taking a sip of wine and then a bigger sip, Tanner started to feel uneasy watching him. "Brint, is everything ok?" "Yes, I'm fine." Pausing, he then took another sip of wine.

Becoming anxious, which was not a feeling, Tanner was used

to, she worked to embrace the feeling and took a sip of her wine. "Tanner?" Brint said with question in his tone. "Is this how it's going to be?" he asked. "Going to be, what exactly do you mean?" she said. "You know, the routine of I go to work, you go to work, we check in at the end of the day just to see if we will see each other in the evening. We come home, eat dinner, sit on the couch, and then go to bed. Then, you know, get up and do it all again the next day," he said.

This was not the conversation that Tanner thought they would be having! Completely taken off guard, she sat staring at her plate wondering how to answer this question.

In the back of her mind, she knew that this was the routine that many couples fell into. It was real, and it didn't resemble any Hallmark Movie she had ever seen. However, she also knew the depth of the love that her grandparents had shared, and her parents, and she never once thought that it looked the way that Brint had just painted it.

"I believe that we both have demanding careers, that we are equally dedicated to, and we both have an understanding of this, and this is the first reason that we work. The second reason we work is that we love each other unconditionally. The third reason we work is that we both are considerate of each other's time. We understand that there is time that is spent together, and that is special and there is time spent with our friends and there is time that is spent by us, and all are equally important to who we are and who we are together. Don't you agree? We are a team, and we support each other. We get through the tough times and enjoy the good times as long as they last and take each day as it comes," she explained. "Tan, everything you say is so right and so, so usual. Do you believe that we have what it takes for the long haul?" he asked. "I just described the long haul!" she said slightly raising her voice. "Oh no! No! No, this is not happening, you are getting cold feet, you?" Now completely rambling, her heart feeling like she had just finished a marathon, beginning to feel a bit lightheaded, she continued. "This is the stuff that happens, wedding a week away, family coming in and the next thing I know I will be standing at the altar, and you will be nowhere to be found!" she said.

Cutting her off abruptly, Brint placed his hand on her hand, "Hey, hey, hey, calm down I just asked a question," he said. "This is not happening!" Tanner demands. "Sweet, nothing is happening. I am simply asking a question," Brint said. "Well, it's not like we are looking up at the stars and dreaming about what our future will hold," she said. "Maybe I should not have stated it like I did. It came out completely wrong. Maybe I should not have brought this up at all, it's just that I was talking with Andy at lunch today, and he said I needed to talk to you. You are my best friend, and best friends they talk, right? Isn't that what best friends do?" he said. "Wait you talked to Andy, mister love-'em' and leave-'em,' third time's a charm! You talked about THIS to him. This has been on your mind, and I am just now being let in on the secret, this issue," she said. "Tan, it's not a secret and it certainly isn't an issue!" Brint said.

Tanner pushed her plate away and stood from the table, taking her wine glass with her, she walked outside. The lack of food in her belly and the feeling of her blood pressure rising, she could not find her center. "Tanner, wait!" Coming up behind her, he wrapped his arms around her waist as to keep her from running although there was nowhere to go on the balcony. He tightened his embrace and turned her toward him. Taking the glass of wine from her hand, placing it on the table, he grasped her hands in his. Pulling them to his heart, leaning his forehead against hers, he looked deep into her eyes. Deliberately, he held her tight. Brushing his lips against hers, he could feel her start to soften her stance. He, too, began to relax as they both began swaying with the breeze that was whirling around them.

Communicating with their body language he now held her face gently in his hands, brushing her cheekbones with his thumbs ever so slightly, he bent to kiss her now quivering lip. Cupping his lips around hers. She grabbed him pulling him toward her. She did not want to let go. Tanner could feel him responding to her intention. They clumsily found their way inside as she pulled his shirt from his jeans and up over his head. Sweeping Tanner from her feet, he took back a little power that she stole to seduce him. He walked toward their bedroom and gently laid her down. Delicately he kissed her. He stopped to gaze at this beautiful woman beneath him. Listening to her breath was satisfying. The slower he moved the quicker her breath became. He raised his head to see the pleasure on her face. One hand behind her head and the other behind her hip. Brint wanted to show her the love he felt for her. Telling her felt meaningless.

Whispering in her ear, "Sweet, this is the feeling I want you to have when you look at me. This is the feeling I want you to know with all your mind, body, and soul," he said as he stared deep into her eyes. "This is us! We are right for each other, we work together, we fit together. There will always be a tough time, but with you I know we can get through them," he said passionately. "Yes," Tanner replied with a gentle sigh. "I'm sorry for doubting us. I have had some questions, too," Tanner said, her voice gaining a little more control. "You have?" he responded with an understanding in his voice that calmed her immediately. "Yes, when I didn't come home right away the other night, I took a drive, and I had some things I had to deal with," she explained. "Like what?" he asked. "You know you can tell me anything. I mean anything and I am here to listen. If it bothers you, it matters to me," he said. "You know stuff, the past, the present. I just had to find my center again," she said as she tried to lower her head. Placing his finger over her lips, he rolled toward her, cradling her head gently in his hand, he began to kiss her again. Feeling safe in one another's embrace they fought the urge to give in to their desire.

CHAPTER 4

Uncovering

As the elevator doors opened, he was greeted by the light gray marble floors and the misted glass reception desk. "Good morning, Mr. Winstead," she said. Merritt was always pleasant to see and hear in the morning. It was part of the routine that started his day out on the right foot. She was sophisticated but sweet. This morning, she had her thick, dark, brown hair pulled back in a ponytail, showing off her cheekbones and defined jawline. Clint thought to himself, she must be royalty, I am sure of it. She is exquisite and smart too. Stopping at the desk, he asked for any messages. Handing them to him, she paused before handing the last one to him. "Mr. Winstead? This one is different. The lady that left it would not leave her name or number," Merritt stated. "Really?" Clint asked. Thinking for a moment, he stared out the window of the 23rd floor. "What did she sound like?" he asked. "Sir, she was very proper, she had a southern accent," she said. Knowing exactly who she was talking about, a smile crept across his face as he took the note from her. "Thanks!" Clint turned toward his office. Merritt noticed almost a skip in his step. Thinking to herself, that is what he deserves. His crooked smile gave it all away!

Merritt had worked with Clint for the last six years. He gave her a chance that no one else had. So, she was forever grateful. He took the time to interview her for what she could bring to the office and not just a pretty face to decorate the lobby. She knew exactly what she was doing when it came to research, she had an open mind and often helped Clint think outside of the box. She made each client feel special and taken care of. Often times, they would call into the office and be completely frantic. By the time she hung up with them, they were calm and confident.

Merritt gathered the files she had been working on and took them to Clint's office, her daily routine. She laid the files on the corner of the desk. As Merritt turned with her usual confidence, she started out the door. Just before it closed, Clint requested that she reschedule his afternoon meeting and informed her that he would be leaving at noon and would not be returning for the day! Noon came very quickly, and Clint called out to Merritt, "I am leaving now, I will see you in the morning."

Clint started his car, and the hum of the engine made him feel confident and bit powerful. The quote, "Today's the day," had been stuck in his head since he left his apartment this morning. The thought of her made him smile. The thought of actually seeing her made him weak. The thought of never seeing her again made him sad. The thought of tearing her apart in a courtroom made him feel powerful and triumphant, but so did tearing anyone apart in a court of law. The thought of touching her brought him back to reality. "Never!" he said out loud. Never again because it would tear his heart out, never again because he knew he would never again get the time of day or never again because he slammed on the breaks! He had put the car in reverse and didn't realize he was slowly rolling backward. The alarm startled him as a passing car drove behind him, and it quickly brought him out of the daze he had drifted into.

Pulling out of the parking garage, he turned toward the park. All he could think about was getting his head cleared, so he could make some especially important, possibly life changing decisions. The only place he could think of to do this was the park. The park where it all started. Finding a safe place to leave his Mercedes, he headed toward the fountain. Sitting on the bench where they shared so many thoughts, feelings, tears, and laughter he found himself start to unwind. Closing his eyes, he slowly took a deep breath and let it out even slower. Thinking to himself, "I refuse to face her in court. I refuse. I can't." It wasn't the thought of possibly losing this time, it was a more precious thought which surprised him, it really wasn't his nature.

However, when it came to Tanner, she brought out something deep in him.

CHAPTER 5
Time Away

As the morning light started to peek through the blinds, Tanner began to stir in the sheets. Feeling the slight movement, Brint rolled over and brushed the hair from her face. Not saying a word, he pulled her toward him and gently squeezed her. There were those times when they never had to exchange a single word, but they could have a complete conversation just the same. They laid there for what seemed like hours although the clock reflected about ten minutes had lapsed. She looked at Brint, and praying to herself, "God, please let him understand what I am about to say. I want you to know that I love you with all my heart. I want to spend the rest of my life with you. I mean it with everything I have to offer you. I am going to go for my dress fitting today, then I'm heading to Tennessee for a few days. I don't want you to worry. I really need to spend some time by myself. It's mostly to prep for the Copeland case. But I need my roots. I need I just know I need to go," she said, pleading gently.

Feeling his stomach tighten, he felt that burning feeling that one feels just before they start to shed tears from deep within. Using all the energy he had gained this morning to hold back that horrible feeling, he did his best to take a deep breath, and think clearly enough to say what was right. He knew that she was vulnerable, and he needed to be tender with her and respectful of her feelings. He knew she was a strong woman and if she felt she needed something, it was right and true. "Will you go to the lake house?" he questioned. "Yes," she assured him. "Do your mom and dad know you are going?" he inquired. "Yes," said Tanner. "Will you be there by yourself?" he asked. "Yes," she reassured him again. "Is that safe?" he asked. "C'mon, it's Norris," she reminded him. "I know, I just," he agreed with hesitation. "Stop! I will be fine," she argued. "I know, but when will I be able to expect you home? Home, here, with me," he asked pressingly.

The confusion building in Brint's voice started to come through. "Did I do something? I must ask?" said Brint with concern. "No! Please. I am good. We are good," Tanner explained. Brint knew her well enough that when she ended with an I am good statement, he knew something was stirring. However, she would not let him, or anyone else know. He knew her well enough to know that she would let it stir like a hurricane, until it made its way far from her thoughts. He also knew that he would probably never know what those thoughts were, what they meant, or where they went when they left. What he did know was, once they were gone, they were gone.

"So, you will leave after your fitting? Does your sister know?" "Yes, she knows!" Hearing the frustration coming through her words, he paused. Thinking to himself, "So everyone knows, and I am the last to find out. I don't think I will go there with that. That will ignite a fire." "OK, I just know that I love you. I love you with all my being. I will be here waiting anxiously for you and" Touching his lips gently to keep them from moving, she kissed her finger, and placed it over his lips. She rolled out of bed and headed to the bathroom. She did what she called throwing herself together, although, Brint thought she looked like a million dollars. Her hair was thrown up in a messy bun. She had on a pair of light blue slacks with a pair of sandals. She had on a pale, lemon yellow, linen shirt that lit up her face. She's so beautiful, he thought to himself. She blew him a kiss as she flew out the door.

CHAPTER 6

A Meeting To Remember

Bring finished his shower and poured himself a cup of coffee. Stepping out on the balcony of their fifteen-story building, he could see for what seemed like forever. The buildings looked as if he could jump from one to another, up and down, high, and low. It was a beautiful sight. The small patches of greenway and groves of trees made him feel alive. He loved his city. The breeze coming from Lake Michigan on this September morning was crisp and refreshing. He was born and raised in Chicago and could never imagine leaving. He loved the pace of this magnificent city. It had so much to offer and could satisfy any mood you could be in. The rain had finally come to pass, and the birds were still singing.

Taking a sip from his coffee mug and then filling his lungs with air put him at ease for the first time in the last few hours. Doing his best to push all negative thoughts aside, he sat on the lounge chair. He pulled the Chicago Tribune from under his arm and began to scan the first page when an article caught his eye. Copeland Proper-ties, CFO before Brint could finish reading the headline, his mind was going a hundred miles an hour in all directions.

He sat up. Placing his coffee cup on the table beside him, he began reading.

> *"CFO, Leonard S. Copeland was found unresponsive and pronounced dead in his home in Lincoln Park Friday morning. Cause of death has not been determined. A pending investigation is in progress."*

Lowering the paper, he looked across the vast real estate in front of him. Realizing that the majority of the buildings within eyesight were managed or owned by Copeland Properties, this was a huge deal. Jumping up from his chair, he dashed inside grabbing his phone from the kitchen island and he called Tanner. The call immediately went to voice mail. "Hi, this is Tanner Bingham with The Bingham Forester Law Firm. I am unable to take your call at this time. Please leave your name, number and a brief message and I will return your call as soon as possible," Tanner's voicemail resounded, "T this is B; You need to call me as soon as you get this message! Something has happened with your case, and you need to know!" he said looking at his phone, the picture of Tanner staring back at him made his heart start to race. Feeling his legs turn to jelly, he slowly walked to the couch and sat. He just realized Tanner had left with a kiss blown in his direction, and she had disappeared around the corner. How could he have just let her go like that? He was usually the one leaving abruptly without much information. The word payback came to mind.

He quickly brushed the thought aside knowing Tanner would never do something intentional to hurt him or their relationship, so he moved on. He stepped back outside, and the temperature already felt as if it were a few degrees warmer than just five minutes before, he grabbed his coffee cup, shut, and locked the door behind him and walked to the sink. Placing his mug beside hers, he stood there staring. Her mug beside his, his mug beside hers. It was comforting to see a glimpse of their life together. He found peace again in this small moment and turned toward the bedroom. Sitting on the stool in their closet, he reached for his running shoes. Again, there were her shoes, hers beside his and his beside her reflections of the things they enjoyed doing together. He stopped for a moment to remember the day that they met.

It was a hot, August evening. Both were running on the Lakefront Trail when a small boy on a bicycle popped a wheelie and couldn't recover. The boy crashed to the ground with his bike landing on top of him! They found themselves knelt beside him with the boy's mother looking for broken bones and looking over a few scratches. He remembered how sweet Tanner was to the little boy and how gentle she was as she touched him. The sweet, gentle sound of her southern draw made even him feel calm after witnessing such an event.

After the little boy was back on his bike and speeding away, his mother chasing and calling after him to slow down, they turned to each other and laughed. "Kids?" Brint said, shaking his head. Without missing a beat, he looked into the warm brown eyes and continued, "Remember when we were kids, we didn't wear helmets, knee pads, or elbow pads. If I had pulled that stunt, I would have been bleeding from head to toe and suffered a minor concussion. Of course, I would have still jumped on my bike and rode off into the sunset just as he just did! I am sorry, here I am rambling on, my name is Brint, Brint McClendon," he said, holding out his hand. Tanner shook it replying, "I am Tanner, Tanner Bingham."

Brint quickly noticed the last name, Bingham. Being in his field, he was familiar with all the top and upcoming attorneys. "Bingham, as in Bingham and Forester?" Tanner confidently replied. "Yes!" "I work in the States Attorney's office and for this reason for that reason, we know," he said. She could tell he was trying to explain away the awkward, so she put her hand up and with a smile said, "I understand."

Without realizing, it they were strolling side by side along the lake front sharing stories. An hour later, Tanner was back at her starting point and Brint, embarrassed to say, was several miles in the opposite direction. Tanner offered to drive him to his car. He quickly took her up on her offer.

With a smile, she turned on the vehicle and the stereo blasted to life blaring 38 Special, "Wild-Eyed Southern Boys." The first words he heard were...'

But he doesn't stand a chance in hell, 'cause he ain't no wild-eyed Southern boy.' He remembered thinking to himself, appropriate. It was all too obvious that Tanner was from the South.

On the short drive back to his car, he could barely pay attention to any of the words she spoke. He was too busy trying to think of a way to get her number and ask for another chance to talk to her. As she turned in to the lot, he interrupted her in mid-sentence, blurting out, "Do you drink coffee?" Tanner could not help herself. She pulled her car into a parking spot, put her car in park, leaned back in her seat, turned her head toward him with a tilt and a small smirk across her lips. She chuckled and said, "I was just telling you about the new little coffee shop down the street from my building."

Chuckling to herself this time, she watched a smile crawl across his face. Brint remembered feeling the blood flow immediately to his cheeks, and he could not help but bust out into laughter. He remembered thinking to himself; this girl has got me. From the first moment I was in her presence, she's got me. "Tanner, to be very honest with you," said Brint as he paused a moment to look into her eyes. Brint marveled to himself, "Milk chocolate, sweet eyes, I think you see right through me. I think you are going to make me amuse myself in my own presence." He continued in the present to answer her, "I did not hear a word that you said." "Not a word?" asked Tanner. "No," he said in laughter. "Not one word. I was too busy trying to figure out how I was going to ask you for your number to invite you to coffee tomorrow morning," explaining himself to her. The car filled with laughter! He began tying his shoe, he sighed. Standing with more energy from the fond memory, he made his way through their apartment and down to his car.

CHAPTER 7

The Getaway Cabin

Tanner sat cradled comfortably by the seat of her car and the seat belt was fastened snugly. She had driven over halfway in a matter of hours. Seeing the blue sign ahead that read "Welcome to Kentucky," she relaxed a bit. She knew in approximately three and a half hours she would be pulling down the gravel road to the cabin. Needing to get out and walk a bit she took the next exit and pulled into the busiest gas station she could find. She felt safer with more people around. Her mother and father had always given her the rules of safe travel before each trip. Memorized now, this was around number five or six on the list. Texting her mom to let her know what exit she was on and what station she was at would record the place and time of her last known whereabouts.

She bought a bottle of water and a snickers bar which were her travel favorites. She filled up her tank and was back on the road in no time. The ring of her phone screaming through the speakers startled her. She always loved it when her mom's cheerful picture showed up on the tiny screen on her dashboard. She pressed the phone button on the steering wheel and in a peppy voice said, "Hey mamma! I am back on the road, I forgot to text you when I got back in the car. I am just anxious about getting there." "I know honey, I just knew you had taken long enough and figured that is what had happened, so you know me, I had to call," explained Madeline. "I know, I am a big girl now, you don't have to worry so much, although, I know that you will. It's what you do," said Tanner. "Yes, it is!" said Tanner's mom. "I am about three hours out. I should be there in time for supper," she said. "Hon, I spent the afternoon sprucing up the cabin, I left some groceries there for you, but I am beat. I didn't cook anything. Call me when you get there, and then we can catch up tomorrow. I had your dad cut some kindling and there is dry wood on the porch. I thought you might want to build a fire," said Madeline. "Mom, you are too sweet. Thank you for getting me set up. Tell daddy thank you for the wood. I will call when I get there, promise," said Tanner. "You better, or you know what I will do," said mamma with a laugh. "Yes, Unfortunately, I do know what you will do. That's the last thing I need is the police showing up at my door," said Tanner sarcastically. "It's just because I love you dear." "I love you mom. I will talk to you shortly."

As she hung up, her stereo blared to life, awakening a deep but familiar nostalgia that lived inside her. It was part of her soul. This was a part of her that made her feel unique. There were only a couple of close friends that understood this part about her and of course her mother. She wished that she could share this piece with her sister, but she could never get her to focus seriously enough to completely understand.

It was a place she retreated to renew herself, to laugh, and to find happiness. It was sometimes to conquer a sadness that was present in the depths of her being. She felt herself grip the steering wheel a bit tighter, pushing herself back in her seat as she pressed the gas pedal a bit more. She could feel the sun beaming through the cracked sunroof, warming her skin. She was feeling quite confident in her moment. "Runnin' out of self- control, Gettin' close to an overload, up against a difficult situation, Shoulder to shoulder, push and shove, I'm hangin' up my boxin' gloves, I'm ready for a long vacation."

Singing at the top of her lungs, she found additional confidence from Journey's, Be Good to Yourself. A song that had pushed her through several moments in her past that proved to be so insignificant now, but at the time were the end of the world as she knew it. Her mind drifted to a quick trip to Atlanta with her bestie. A time when it was a fun pastime to feel a bit defiant. Catching a glimpse of her speed, she chuckled and decided she better slow down. Getting pulled over out of state was never a good idea.

CHAPTER 8
Frazzled

Feeling a change in the temperature, Clint realized that the sun was setting. He shook his head in disbelief. Thinking to himself, "How long have I been sitting here? What has come over me?" Staring across the park, he took a mental note of the couples sitting here and there, and then there was the couple walking hand in hand by the fountain. As the young man slowed, then turned to the young girl, Clint found himself mesmerized. "Is he going to kiss her? No, no kiss, he thought to himself. Stop!" screamed Clint. The couple jerked at the sound of Clint's voice, turning in his direction and chuckling among themselves, Clint realized he had done it yet again.

In the past couple of weeks, Clint had noticed himself answering his thoughts aloud. This was something he did when he was frazzled his mother had once pointed out to him. "Frazzled," Clint called himself. The couple turned and looked in his direction again, this time with a look of concern on their face. Thinking to himself this time, "I did it again!"

Springing to his feet, he stood up and headed to his car. When he started his car, he sat trying to think of his next move. Without further pause, he called her office. He quickly hung up. Putting his car in drive he turned toward home. Instead of going directly home this evening, he decided to stop by Dale's. Before he made it all the way through the door, Jeff looked up from the bar and immediately reached for a highball glass and Clint's favorite.

Clint walked over to his regular spot at the bar and loosened his tie. "Rough day buddy?" said Jeff. Clint looked into his glass, cupping it slightly, he lifted it to his lips and took a gulp. As he was placing his glass back on the bar, he looked up. He saw his reflection in the mirror behind the bar, he made notice that he really didn't look himself. Looking back down, as if to avoid eye contact, he mumbled, "Yeah" with a bit of a sigh mixed in with the response. Jeff quickly filled his glass back to its original level. "Do you feel like talking about it?" asked Jeff.

Clint had been so busy building his career, that he had lost all contact with his college buddies. He didn't want friends in his field. It wasn't smart. He spoke to his father quite frequently, his secretary and Jeff. Jeff would be considered his best friend if guys were even to have best friends. He found himself confiding in Jeff from time to time.

Without pause, Clint started, "Jeff, have you ever had something get a hold of you, a hold of your mind. Hell, a hold of your soul that kept you so off track you started talking to yourself?" "You mean, like a girl?" asked Jeff. "Well, yeah!" with an edgy sting in his voice, Clint sharply replied. Then thinking to himself, what the hell else would I be talking about? "Women are about the only species that can drive you to drink and make you go plain nuts!" said Clint taking a sip of his drink. He stared down at the mahogany bar longing to figure this out with Tanner. Looking at the many scratches, tracing a few with his finger, he threw down a twenty and stood from his bar stool. "Man, I'll see you later. I need to call it a night," said Clint. Jeff had seen that look before. In his profession, it was something that he knew all too well. He thought to himself that Clint was about to do something out of character.

CHAPTER 9
Traveling Home

Tanner, rounding the curves on Jellico, focused on her driving but her mind was in full force. The sun was beginning to fade after a long day and so was she. It was her, the road, wind from the sunroof and the radio. The sinking sun in her review mirror brought about this nostalgia that was like a hand reaching in her soul and giving it a tight squeeze. It always did that to her and especially this time of year. There was nothing closer to her center than the sinking sun in the South.

She flipped the song and without warning she hears," keep *it all inside,* don't *show how much she rocked ya,*" by the Blues Travelers. Fading in the background and memories that came rushing back were almost too much to handle, but without fail, she was suddenly beside him. Driving down a winding road to what felt like nowhere, the sound of the harmonica blared through the speakers. They had woven their way to and fro through the back roads of

Tennessee and ended up on the Blue Ridge Parkway. Neither one exchanging words, just being there together experiencing the breathtaking scenery was more conversation than one could truly take in. That was the thing. They could be doing nothing or something and it was everything." Can you feel the same, gotta love the pain, looks like rain again, can you feel it comin' in, the mountains win again."

Just then, she popped back into her current reality. She could not help but think about the words, something she did often. Music always guided her in some way from the time she was a little girl. Between the majestic view in her rear-view mirror, the song on the radio and the feeling in the pit of her stomach, she was about spent. She pressed the pedal a bit harder. Looking at her navigation, she was about forty-five minutes out and regulated her speed accordingly to knock that down as quickly as possible. She knew that if she could just make it through the front door, she would be safe from memories and from herself. She had learned over the years that she could self-sabotage in a nanosecond.

Seeing her exit ahead, she slowed, turned on her blinker and took a deep breath. "Almost home," she thought.

She was winding her way through Norris, thinking, "Just a few more turns, and I am there." She could feel the temperature drop as she neared the lake. The air was fresh and crisp. She filled her lungs as she pulled down the long, winding, gravel road leading to her parent's cabin. As she veered right, there it was. It was well manicured, as her dad would not have it any other way. Her senses told her he grasses had been recently mowed.

As she continued down the narrow, gravel drive, she spotted a couple of deer to her left. She slowed; she did not want to disturb dinner. They raised their head to check her out. Standing like statues, she crept by. When the deer felt they were out of harm's way, they went back to munching on the grass.

Placing her car in park, she paused. Looking toward the lake and seeing the sun's reflection, she, too, sat as still as a statue. She could hear a motorboat in the distance, but she heard the birds chirping. Tanner heard the wind rustling the leaves on the trees. She could feel a slight breeze. She filled her lungs again. It almost felt as if she had been holding her breath for the last eleven and a half hours. She released the deep breath and with it the pent-up anxiety that felt like it had the weight of an x-ray blanket.

Opening her door and stretching her legs, she took in another deep breath. She could not get enough. Taking in the smell of lake water, the flowers still in bloom, the distant scent of a fire, and every other smell she could embrace, she did her best to commit them to her soul. Although, they were already there, she called upon them often. She walked toward the front porch. There was a white pitcher by the front door with an arrangement of fresh flowers. White daisies were her favorite, with a hint of baby's breath and some greenery. Certain her mother had placed them there, she looked at them and smiled. Her mother always had a way of reminding her that she was there even when she was not physically present. She pushed the door open, and her senses sprung to life once more. The faint smell of smoke from the fireplace and the damp smell from the woods developed her. She loved everything about this place. She was finally in her safe space. Safe from her past, present, and future.

CHAPTER 10

Thinkin' Problem

Brint had been staring at the clock since he returned from his run. He had tried to read and found that impossible. He had even begun to dial her number a couple of times and pressed the glaring red button just before it began to ring. He knew he needed to contact her. He had to fill her in on the morning headline.

All of a sudden, he felt so overwhelmed and was unable to make a decision. Deep down he knew that she needed her space. This was super important. He knew that she had been extremely focused on the case.

Suddenly his thoughts paused. "You idiot!" he exclaimed aloud. Thinking to himself, "You have not one time asked her why it was so important? Why did she seem so distant? What was so important about this case versus the many others that she seemed to crush in court without so much as a blink of the eye?" Brint continued to ask himself these questions. She was used to winning. She usually did. He had never asked who she was up against, only the basics. Their conversation always was from the thirty-thousand-feet level when it came to work. Mostly because he had to keep his so secretive. But that didn't mean they couldn't share a bit more. As it was, they spent more time with their careers than with one another.

He decided to calm his spinning mind. He poured himself a glass of wine and headed toward the porch to relax. As he drew a deep breath, he threw himself into the lounge chair on the porch. He could not keep her from his thoughts. Brint felt like a jerk, and he was missing her terribly. Watching the sun set, he felt the breeze now much cooler rustle through his hair. The buildings casting their shadows across the land like a dark blanket. One by one the lights of the city flickered to life. The different colored streetlights, lights left on over the weekend in the buildings and the blinking lights on the top of the buildings to warn aircraft began their rhythm. Hypnotizing as it was, it didn't bring him relaxation this evening as it usually did. He just needed to hear her voice.

Clint returned home, opened the door to an empty room silence and darkness. Flipping the light switch, he threw his keys in the matte silver basket with a clang. He walked to the patio doors. Opening them, he finally felt life, even if it was that of a refreshing lonely breeze. Filling his lungs, he stepped outside. Leaning against the concrete railing, he rubbed his face, raising his head, stopping just short, his fingertips just below his eyes, he blinked. Thinking to himself, "You have to take control if you want something to happen." Control. It's something he was a little too good at. He thought to himself, "I feel so confused, so overwhelmed. Am I even worthy of such a precious gem?" He stood there staring. Breeze blowing, the horns honking he knew that there was plenty of life going on without him. He turned to go back inside and felt somber. He didn't bother fixing a drink this evening. Stopping in the bathroom to wash the day off and change, he went straight to bed. Laying there, he began his conversation again. I need her. I want her. He didn't wrestle too much tonight as he was very well medicated with liquor.

CHAPTER 11

Smothering Peace

Tanner pulled out her phone, dialing her mom. "Hey mom, I am home," said Tanner as she was unpacking. "Oh pumpkin, I was just thinking that you should be arriving any time now. I am so glad that you made it safely," said Madeline. She hated it when her mom called her pumpkin, or pumpkin-eater. She quickly reminded herself that one day she might long to hear that very dreaded word and give anything for it. So, she complied. "I am going to get settled in and I will call you tomorrow afternoon placing emphasis on after noon," said Tanner.

Remembering a time when she was about twenty-three. She had left work on time and called her grandma on the way home. Searching for something else to do as she was tired of the loud bars and the uneasy feeling, she always had there. She was never able to let loose anyway. She was always on guard for her own protection always questioning the intentions of those who approached her.

So, tonight, she decided to keep herself grounded by going to her grandmother's. Not even thinking to check in with her mother, she hurried home, packed a small overnight bag, and headed back out the door. She took her time driving enjoyed her time alone and listened to her favorites on the radio. Tanner was so caught up that she was startled by her phone buzzing, so she answered quickly. She heard her mother's frantic voice on the other end. "Tanner, where have you been?" screamed Madeline. It was a scared, scolding tone that made her shrink. She never wanted to disappoint anyone, especially her mother. "I have called your work, and they said you left three hours ago. I called the police, and they have knocked on your apartment door with no answer. Where are you young lady?" Tanner's mother nervously asked.

Explaining her events and intentions of her evening, she thought her mother might feel much better knowing she wasn't 'clubbing' this evening it might change her mood. To no avail, she kept pleading her case. Finally, her mother hung up, stating that she was calling the police back to let them know that I had been found. Thinking to herself, "I never knew I was lost!" Hanging up the phone, she turned up her radio and drowned herself in music. She always did this when she felt like she wanted to get away or completely disappear from her life. She played one of her favorites" Runnin' on self-control, gettin close to an overload, up against a no-win situation." Journey was definitely a go-to.

Tanner had to bring herself back to the present. She went to the cupboard to find the tea. Her mom always had her favorite on hand, Constant Comment, Orange Spice. Filling the copper kettle that was always kept on the stove, she filled it with water and waited for it to boil. She opened up the refrigerator and found that her mom had already made one of her favorite dishes. Goulash was comfort food for sure. All she had to do was heat it in the microwave.

Dishing out a small portion, the kettle started singing. She filled a pitcher with the perfect number of tea bags and drenched them with the boiling water. After pouring herself a glass, she took her meal to the screened in porch, filling her lungs once more, took a bite, and made sure all taste buds were alive. She sat in silence. The night was slowly coming alive. The crickets she picked out first. Then she heard the croaking of several frogs, big and little. They were beginning to talk to one another. She could hear the gentle splashing of the lake water up against the rocks. Her mind was at complete peace.

CHAPTER 12

From A Distance

Brint made the relutant decision to wait to call. It wasn't like it was going to change the situation by her knowing. She was doing what needed to be done, and he just needed to let her do it. He told himself that he was being supportive. He just needed to be patient and wait for her return. Out of all the difficult, sometimes death-defying, situations he had been put in by his career of choice, he had never felt such anxiety such uncertainty. He knew what to do in those situations, but this, this was horrible. He had never felt the way he did when he was with Tanner. This is the sole reason that he had asked her to marry him. He knew with his whole being that he did not want to live life one more day without her by his side.

This was proof. This was absolute confirmation that he had made the right choice. Watching the hours click by on the clock was just misery in every sense of the word. He sat in his recliner, staring at the cat cleaning herself. "I can't keep on like this. I am going to go crazy. Maybe I already am," he thought. He finally broke down and called her sister. It wasn't Tanner, but it would do. Alexa and Tanner were close, and they always seemed to know when the other needed them even if they had not talked in days weeks. She would be able to create some peace, at least enough to get him through this time. He knew that they would have talked at the dress fitting. She would have the scoop.

Hearing the phone ringing in his ear, he glanced at the clock, and thought to himself, it's only 8:30 p.m., where is she? Surely, her plane would have landed by now, and she would be able to talk. The phone rang and rang. "Hi there, you have reached Lexi's cell phone, and I am not able to answer. Please leave me a message, and I will call you back the first chance I get," Lexi's voicemail continued, but Brint ended the call abruptly, and sank in his chair. What in the world was he supposed to do to fill this current void? He was really perplexed now.

He turned on the fireplace and flipped on the CD player. "Oh boy," he said. It was the CD he had placed in there from the other evening. It, too, seemed to have so many questions left unasked and, yet so many answered at the same time. He quickly changed to something different. Still, completely unsatisfied, he turned it off with frustration. Not knowing what to do next, he tried Lex "Just one more time," he told himself. Still, no answer, and he chose not to leave a message.

Standing up abruptly (he scared the cat half to death), he headed to the bedroom, and pulled back the covers. Wrestling himself into a semi- comfortable position, he felt something strange. It felt like paper. He raised from his pillow, pulling out the small piece of paper. It read, "Good night, I love you, sweet dreams," followed by her personal signature TTF, and an exclamation point with a heart for the dot and her T. She signed all of her letters in this special way. His heart skipped a beat, and he shook his head. "TTF," he said out loud, "Today, Tomorrow, forever." It was just what he needed.

He laid there staring at her sweet note and her empty pillow for what seemed like hours. Finally, he rolled over turning out the light, placing her note where he would see it first thing in the morning. He then snuggled back in bed pulling her pillow close to him. He could smell her scent. A special scent that was combined of her shampoo, perfume, and her skin. It was a delectable mixture that made him feel close, or as close as he was going to get, at this time. It found a way to calm him and make him feel very secure. This, too, was something that she did that no other had and again confirmed his feelings. This was one of the first signs he remembered, provoking thought of a forever future together.

CHAPTER 13

Dying To Get Your Number

Clint had become a very successful attorney, and he had several interns in charge of the 'dirty' work. He didn't work on the weekends any longer. So, he took his shower, taking his time. Upon stepping out, he dried and brushed his teeth, but did not bother to shave or fix his hair. He threw on a pair of khaki shorts and a polo shirt with some leather flip-flops. Clint did not care that his legs had no tan left, and he really didn't care about much of anything except for figuring out a way to personally get to Tanner.

He went to the front door to find his newspaper. There it was neatly rolled as usual. He stopped by the kitchen and poured himself a glass of grapefruit juice. He put a bagel in the toaster. While waiting for it to pop up, he unrolled his paper. Immediately distracted by the headline, he never heard his bagel pop up, he left his juice on the counter and retreated to his kitchen table. He pulled out the chair without taking his eyes off of the headline. He was in a bit of shock, making sure he read it correctly, he started back at the beginning.

Clint laid the paper down and his mind entered a whirlwind state. Looking up from the paper, he slowly turned his head looking at the view.

Soaking in the fact that the view in front of him was owned by his client. His longtime client was gone, dead. He had a million questions running through his mind.

Slowly getting up from the table, he went to his home office and dialed the work office. Putting the phone to his ear, all he could think of was Leo. Clint had developed a close relationship with Leonard Copeland over the years. His father had introduced him as soon as he had graduated from law school and joined the firm. Leo and his father Leonard were their largest clients. Over the years, there had been dinner parties, tennis matches, and a lot of laughter. He and Leo played tennis a couple times a month, weather permitting. He had been to dinner with Leo and his wife, and always envied how put together his life seemed to be. Clint always dreaded dinner invitations because he had no idea whom to take with him.

Breaking the silence, "Winstead and Associates," Janae, the weekend operator answered. "Janae!" Clint said. "Connect me to McDonald!" Gregory McDonald was his lead associate, and they worked closely together. "Did you see the paper?" asked Clint. "AHH, yeah, I was just getting ready to ring you!" Gregory replied. They both sounded breathless. Shock had just about paralyzed both of their vocal cords. "Have you talked to Leo?" asked Clint. "No, I don't know what to say," said Gregory. Do you know, have you heard, do they suspect foul play?" asked Clint. "I have not heard a word!" replied Gregory. "I am headed to his house. If he calls have him call my cell," requested Clint. He grabbed his keys and was gone in a flash.

All of a sudden, he thought of Tanner. Did she know? He called her office. "Tanner Bingham's Office, how may I help you?" said Sara, Tanner's assistant. "Yes, this is Clint, Clint Winstead," he addressed himself. Before he could finish, Sara just fell short of rudely interrupting. "Clint, yes sir, how may I help you?" she asked. Knowing that he was the opposing counsel, she was very alert to every word he was saying. Her curiosity struck her, and suddenly, she was wondering why on earth was he calling, and why was he calling on a Saturday morning? "I need to get in contact with Ms. Bingham immediately!" he demanded. Hearing the urgency in his voice, she was completely engaged. "Sir, Ms. Bingham has gone out of town for a couple of days and should be returning to the office on Tuesday," Sara explained.

She heard a sigh on the other end of the line and then silence. "Mr. Winstead?" she asked. "Yes, yes, I am sorry. I was just thinking," Clint answered her. "Is there something wrong?" asked Sara. "You are familiar with the Copeland Case?" he asked. "Yes, I am. Ms. Bingham has been working on this for some time, I'm sure you are aware," she said. "I am, I am the," intentionally interrupting this time, "the opposing counsel," she said. "Court is next week. I am very familiar," she said confidently. "Then you will know how urgent it is that I speak with Ms. Bingham," he argued. "Like I said, she is out of the office until Tuesday, but I will be glad to e- mail a message to her," said Sara. "Well, in most circumstances that would be great, however, this is a bit different. You see, Leonard Copeland was found dead. She needs to know," he confessed.

Clint knew that there would be protocol for this type of thing, but he also knew that it would give him a reason to get her number and call her. "Oh!" Sara gasped. Clearly startled by the news, she understood the urgency completely. "Well, I guess in this case, I could give you, her number. Maybe I better just e-mail her with your number?" Sara suggested to Clint. This time he cut her off intentionally. "Maybe you can just give me her number. We do go way back, you may or may not know," he explained. "OK," she agreed. Pausing and talking to herself, "She's going to kill me," Sara intended to say under her breath. "What was that? Sara, Sara, she will not. I promise she will completely understand, and I promise to let her know how helpful you have been," Clint reassured. "The number is 865-428-," she was still speaking. It seemed that he hung up before she could even finish." Hanging up the phone, she decided she better let Tanner know. She knew Tanner checked her text messages more frequently when she was away than her e-mail. She tapped out the following words.

Sara: Tanner, CALL ME, URGENT! Clint
called for your number!

CHAPTER 14

Almost A Silent Night

Tanner finished her meal and headed into the kitchen to place her plate in the sink. She decided that she would head down the hallway to her bedroom and run a warm bath. She started the water, mixing the cold and hot, to create the perfect temperature. Tanner decided that she would roll out the two windows that were at the end of the tub. Noticing her mother had placed a favorite candle of hers on the shelf (Midsummer's Night Yankee candle) just to the right of the window; she lit it. The flickering flame looked as if it were dancing to the sound of the wind rustling through the trees and in time with the different sounds of nature. She poured a dab of bubble bath and watched the foam build. Tanner retrieved her robe from the linen closet and a towel.

Her mom was a little fanatic when it came to the cabin. Everyone had their own-colored towels with matching robes. Her chosen color was a light teal. While her sisters were a slate gray like her eyes. Of course, the bathroom linens also coordinated with the bed linens. She chuckled at this characteristic. Shaking her head, she whispered to herself, "Mom!"

She tested the water with her fingertips, swishing the water to and fro.

Perfect, she thought to herself. The windows at the end of the tub were so large that she almost felt as if she were outside. The thick hardwoods and various fir trees brushed up against the windows and provided the perfect amount of privacy. She sank down in the tub to chin level and closed her eyes. She felt the warm water embrace her body from the tips of her toes up to the top of her shoulders. The water temp caused small beads of sweat to form above her brow. She laid there in the peaceful sounds of her world, her whole world at the moment growing completely weightless as every muscle in her body relaxed.

She was brought back to reality when she felt the cool breeze from the lake. The breeze made its way through the window, bringing with it the faint scent of evergreen. She loved the natural smell of the outdoors. It was the smell that brought her peace and helped bring the clarity she would seek on a regular basis. This home brought her a stillness of center peace. Although, she was a bit disoriented and had no idea how long she had been in the tub, but by the looks of her toes, she could guess about thirty minutes or more.

She reluctantly sat up, closing the window, and reached for her towel. She quickly dried and wrapped herself in her robe. Rubbing her hand over the initials embroidered on the robe's right side, she shook her head and smiled. She washed her face, and splashed herself with lukewarm water, and dabbed herself with moisturizer that had a hinted smell of cucumber. Taking in a deep breath, she felt her heartbeat slowly. Staring at the image in the mirror, she blinked. When her eyes opened again, there she was. She made a mental note that she looked like the same girl, but there was something different.

Not willing to take the time to think too deeply about it, she headed to the bedroom. As soon as she flipped the light off, the small night light flickered on. Shaking her head again, thinking to herself, mom. She pulled the covers back, catching a whiff of tide and downy. Yet another reminder that she was home. She always thought that it was odd because she used the same laundry detergent, and it was never as comforting as it was when she was home. She sat down on the bed pulling her night gown from the drawer in the bedside table, knowing right where everything would be. As she dressed, she began to wonder if she was going to be able to go to sleep. Her body told her yes, but her mind told her no.

She went to the kitchen and made herself a cup of chamomile tea it was a staple in her family's kitchen. There were many evening conversations spent between the three girls over a cup of tea. As she sat on the back porch, looking at the moonlight across the water, she kept breathing deeply filling her lungs with air, sipping smalls sips of tea, and trying to calm her mind. Her peaceful moment ended with the ringing of her phone. Annoyed, she walked back into reality and viewed her phone.

CHAPTER 15

A Wake-Up Call

Brint felt like he had been asleep for hours when his phone rang, waking him from what seemed to be a restful sleep. Staring at the clock, he tried to bring the time into focus. 12:21 a.m.! Feeling annoyed now that he didn't need Lexi, he reluctantly answered the phone. Sounding groggy,

"Hey Lex," he answered with a raspy voice.

"Hey buddy, I saw your missed calls and thought I better call back since you didn't leave a message. What's wrong?" she asked. "Nothing, now," he said as he yawned.

"Ah, OK, are you sure? You called me twice," she persisted. "Oh, Lex, this is embarrassing, let me be honest," he confessed clearing his throat.

"Please, it's just me," she said.

"I know, I was missing and worried about T, but I am good now. How did the fitting go?" he said.

"Oh my, she looked absolutely stunning. You will be in shock. She looked like a dream," she answered with excitement.

"I can only imagine at this point. Hey, I really like the current image that has developed in my mind, but I was looking at the paper this morning and read a disturbing headline. The big case that Tanner is working on. You know the Copeland real estate one?" Brint said as he was sitting up in bed with changes in his tone.

"Yes, of course," Lex answered. "Well, he was found dead yesterday. I think Tanner needs to know since this has had her so preoccupied lately. I mean she has been working late, she has been needing to be by herself more than usual, and she's just been, well, just not my T," he said.

"Brint, I think she has been more preoccupied about the opposing counsel than the case itself. She's used to these big real estate issues. Have you heard her mention, Clint?" she asked with a high-pitched voice.

"Clint, yes, he is the attorney for Mr. Copeland. I have lived here my whole life, and I know exactly who he is. I know he and his father usually work with the wealthy, I know that they win," he said with a concerning voice.

"Well, just call Tanner in the morning," she said. "Do you know if she arrived OK?" he asked. "Oh yes, I think mom was blowing up my phone and then hers, making sure all of her chicks were back where they belonged. When I landed, I had three voice-mails from her? You know our mother. Mom said she had talked to her as she was getting back on the interstate around Jellico, I think."

"I'll call her first thing in the morning," he told her. "That will be good, get some sleep," she said. "You too Lex, thanks for talking to me. I think you are going to make a pretty good sister," he said with a chuckle.

"Pretty good, I am the best and don't you forget it!" she said with a laugh. Brint noticed that she sounded just like her sister. Just that, made him feel much better. Speaking to Lex made him feel close to Tanner, but it wasn't, and he decided to dial T's number once more.

CHAPTER 16

Cooking With Emotions

Clint didn't call Tanner right away. He figured that if Sara was a good secretary, she had contacted her quicker than he could dial the number anyway. It was Saturday, and there was absolutely nothing either one of them could do. Questioning the relevancy of the call, he decided he better get his mind together first. There was actually no reason for him to call her. All details would be worked out through the paperwork and due process. He questioned himself. Knowing good and well that he was just using this as an excuse to get her number, to call her, and to have direct contact with her Clint thought to himself.

Clint had spent the day at Leo Copeland's home. Over the years they had become close, and Copeland, Sr. had started turning more and more of the family business over to him. His father had represented the family for over thirty years. They still did not know much about what had happened. The family was in shock and in a state of devastation.

After leaving the house, Clint had stopped at the store, thinking that if he cooked at home this evening, it would keep his mind off of things. After arriving home with his groceries, he put everything away and poured himself his usual. He placed his glass on the counter noticing how lonely it looked. He had noticed this afternoon how each of the Copeland family had comforted each other. Everyone had their part. He began to wonder if something happened to his father, how would his family react and who would be there to comfort him.

This thought really tugged at his heart. He was having a lot of these types of thoughts lately and had not a single bit of a plan in place to fix this deep void. He pulled out the pans that he would need for his meal. Clint chopped the squash, zucchini and onions and washed the red potatoes before he placed them in a pot to boil. After he placed the lightly seasoned chicken in the oven, he retreated to the living room and turned on the stereo. Unable to figure out who he wanted to listen to, he decided to search his Apple Music by mood, Electronic Chill. He thought to himself, what the hell is that, pushing play and hearing the speakers begin thumping a catchy slow beat mixed with some electric sounding beats, he thought this would do.

Stepping outside with his drink in his hand, he drew in a deep breath and let it out slowly. Taking a sip of bourbon, he made a conscious effort to acknowledge each feeling and scent as it slid down the back of his throat. He looked out over the lights and thought he needed to be more intentional with his life. Yes, there were things that had become routine and mediocre. He needed more depth. He told himself that he didn't have enough substance. No, he thought, that's not it. Depth, that's really what I mean. "Depth?" he questioned. "Define that," he told himself out loud.

He began thinking there is truly more to this life. "There is more to me than my appearance. I am this person who walks this earth, and interacts with those who are around, me, and who I'm in contact with throughout the day. I wonder what they see. Do they see I am a smart guy with common sense? I'm a multilayered man," he pondered. "But who exactly are they? You are really getting deep, he thought? Do I seriously know myself? I know that I really liked who I was at the beginning of college. I felt super grounded and loved the way I felt when I was with Tanner. When did that feeling go away?" he continued to ask himself.

Feeling sickened by the memory, he remembered the first time he cheated on Tanner. He remembered how he felt knowing that not one girl, but three girls had made advances toward him in the last few weeks. It made him feel powerful. None of them knew about one another, and that was even more mysterious. This was all new to him, and he realized he couldn't get enough. He remembered he was obsessed with it. He also remembered the sweeter Tanner was to him the more he began to push her away. At first, it was not returning phone calls in a timely manner, then it turned in to not talking to her for a day here and a day there. Eventually it turned in to anger. He was angry because he wanted to keep her but have the others too, and he could not find enough hours in a day to keep it all separate.

His feelings for Tanner began to change. He became annoyed

with her sweetness because it was a jab at how he was acting. He did not want to give up his second life. Clint remembered how Tanner kept trying to accommodate his irritations finding things to blame them on. School was demanding, needing time 'alone,' and needing time with my study groups; she understood. He realized by this time he was giving her absolutely nothing in return, and she was still trying to accommodate that, and it pissed him off. He tried to explain, and the words never came out right.

"Clint, this is your fault," he told himself.

Even though Clint had figured out when his feelings changed and how it changed who he really was, he was taken back at the fact that, that is how he had remained. Why? Clint knew that he liked both, and he loved the fact his personality had lent itself too many successes. He loved the fact he could obtain anyone and anything he wanted. He loved it left little to be handled, or did it? "I am tired of having the mindset of, I must win or else. It hurts people. But it makes me a damn good attorney. That constant mindset has made me a living," he said laughing to himself. "Living!" he said out loud.

Stepping back inside, he could smell each spice separately, and his senses were extremely heightened. He walked in the kitchen, opened the oven, and feeling the heat even seemed more intense. Poking a fork in the potatoes, noting to himself that they were done, he removed them from the stove eye. The veggies had simmered together perfectly, and he turned off the stove and took the chicken out of the oven. He fixed his plate and retreated to the living room. He turned off his music, acknowledging that it wasn't bringing him the feeling he thought it would. He sat, eating in silence.

Hearing himself chew, he acknowledged that this, too, was annoying, and he flipped on the television. The first story to air was about his friend. He quickly flipped that station. He randomly punched the remote. Anything was better than something serious. He was thinking to himself; I am over serious. Choosing to eat slowly this evening instead of liking it was a meal that needed to be had because that is what you did. He found himself relaxing with each bite. Putting together the perfect combination of each fork full, he slowly found his happy place, even if it was just for the moment.

CHAPTER 17

Drama

"Lex, what the, why are you calling me so late? You scared me half to death!" Tanner said.

"I'm sorry, I didn't mean to bother you. I just wanted to let you know that Brint called me," Alexa explained. "He did? Why?" Tanner asked confused about this whole conversation.

"Well, you know the case you have been working on Mr. Copeland died," she said to her.

"What?" she asked frantically.

"Why would Brint call you over that, why wouldn't he just call me?" she demanded. Feeling her blood pressure rise more over the fact Brint had chosen to call Lexi, instead of her. She found herself focused more on the fact that her sister had just told her that her biggest case yet was dead. Stopping herself, "Did you just say, Mr. Copeland died?" she asked to confirm.

"Yes, I did," she said. There was silence on the line. You could hear breathing and crickets, literally. Crickets, as she was back on the porch. "That is what Brint called you about?" she asked again in disbelief. "It was, well I also added how amazing you looked today," she said trying to ease the news of the conversation.

"LEX, Wait! Let me put you on speaker, I need to look this up. So, I am not finding much, did he tell you anything specific?" said Tanner. "No, he

was just concerned and thought you should know. I told him you had probably already heard from Sara, and he should call you in the morning. He sounded a bit desperate," Lexi explained. Laughing to herself,

"Desperate, that is a word that would never describe Brint."

She continued to search her phone for missed calls and texts. "Yikes!" she exclaimed. "Sara called twice and sent me four text messages and an e- mail! This is exactly what I get for trying to find some peace. I should not have come. I just need to go back tomorrow and get back to the office," she said disturbed with this news.

"Tanner! No, you don't! What are you going to do bring him back to life?" Lexi asked with sarcasm. "Hey, that was rude?" said Tanner.

"Well, seriously, what are you going to do? This case has had you screaming in the dark. It has held you at the office all hours of the night. I am sure things will be put on hold for the moment. At least long enough for you to chill out. I have never heard so much tension in your voice. When I saw you, from the outside you appeared so put together, but, T, your voice was tight and airy. I noticed all the signs that tell me you are stressed to the max and that you have way more going on than you have bothered to tell me! Which makes me so angry at you and even more worried about you! Tanner this isn't right. Something is going on," Lexi said with concern.

"What?" Tanner asked. "It's time you quit trying to be my big sister all the time and let me in!" Lexi commanded. "Lexi girl, I am your big sister!" said Tanner. She was the only one that could get away calling her that and Lexi hated it. "Seriously, Tan! I mean it! What is going on with you?" Lexi asked again. "Hang on," Tanner said. Lexi was left holding on the other line. Still, no answers. She was getting angrier by the second.

Brint was calling. Strangely enough, it was as if she was mad that it was him. "Why would she feel that way?" Tanner asked herself. Lex said she told him to call in the morning. Thinking to herself out loud, "I guess he couldn't wait." Trying not to sound so annoyed, she answered, "Hey."

"T, I know that you need your time, but there is something you should know!" he explained as he sounded breathless, nervous, anxious, and a little on edge. This was not a side she was used to hearing of Brint, who was always greatly confident in all situations.

"Yeah, I know! Lex just called," Tanner said. "Hang on, she's on the other line!" she told Brint. Without waiting on a response, she switched lines.

"Hey, Lexi Girl, which is Brint. I'm sure he's calling to tell me what you already have. I will catch up with you. I obviously have some calls to make, and I really need to call Sara. She's been calling, and I missed them all. I bet she's about to wring my neck! Love you!" Tanner said and she ended her call with Lexi. Before Lexi could respond, Tanner switched back to Brint. "Babe, I know why you are calling, as much as I want to talk, I'm going to have to call you back. I need to call Sara she has called a couple of times. I missed all of them!" Tanner explained.

Brint's mood completely deflated! "I really need to talk to you!" Brint declared with desperation. Tanner was taken aback by the sound. "Honey, I will, but I have to call Sara!" Tanner pleaded. "OK, but please call me back!" he asked. Tanner thought, "Good grief." She said it out loud, not realizing she hadn't hung up between the chaos of the moment and the back and forth of conversation between Brint and her sister, she heard, him say,

"What?" Hearing Brint's voice this time with a snip. "Oh! Great!" she thought to herself. Rolling her eyes and throwing her head back in disgust at herself, she started speaking to him again, "Sweet, I didn't mean that! It's just that my first night here has been drama. I was in overload when I left and now this," Tanner replied calmly. "This, what's that mean?" he asked. "No, not you," she reassured him.

Cutting her off he started, "First, we love you, I love you. I tried to stay busy today, and all I can think about is you. Then when I read this article, it," he said pausing to slow himself down. As he thought to himself, he suddenly realized that he sounded frantic and a bit desperate. He sat staring out the window. Looking out into the city lights, he ran his hand through his hair. He took a big breath and started again. "Never mind, listen," he said trying to control his emotions. "I thought you might want to know sooner than later. Honestly, I forgot that you have your people to keep you informed. T, I'm going to let you go for the night. Why don't you get some sleep and pick up on this in the morning if you must?" he said with a sigh of relief.

Tanner appreciated that he was acknowledging her need to get off the phone. She wanted to apologize further for earlier but chose not to, because she just didn't have it in her to explain. "I will. I love you!" he said as he hung up not realizing that she didn't say it back. Brint sat there analyzing her tone and the exchange of words. What made matters worse was he could remember this was the first time she had hung up without saying I love you. All he could think was "She has hung up twice in one day without saying it." Brint walked to the bedroom and collapsed on the bed. He grabbed her pillow and squeezed it tightly. Before he knew it, he was fast asleep and dreaming of a better tomorrow.

CHAPTER 18

Humbling

After finishing his food, he carried his plate to the kitchen. Leaving it in the sink as usual, he sat down at his desk. He reclined in his leather chair. Rocking a bit in the silence and hearing the slight rub of the leather, which made him feel extremely alone, he picked up his pen. When he was in deep thought, on the verge of a breakthrough, he would tap his pen, ink side first, twirl it through his fingers, and tap again. He would do this over and over without missing a beat. Tonight, his thoughts were far from his case. He wanted to figure out a way to somehow apologize to Tanner for the way he treated her. He thought that by doing so it may release him from the grasp she had on him in his sub-conscience mind or even better, open up the door to revisit their friendship again.

He paused briefly to think deliberately about that specific task. "Where do I start?' he mumbled to himself. Out of the silence, he could swear he heard a voice that said, "Humble yourself." It was like his conscience was speaking out loud. For the first time in a really long time, Clint wanted to right all the wrongs in his life. He remembered a verse he had heard a long time ago. 2 Chronicles 7:14, "If My people, which are called by my name, shall humble themselves and pray, and seek my face, and turn from their wicked ways; then will I hear from heaven, and will forgive their sin, and will heal their land".

Clint felt a peaceful feeling come over him. He paused and took notice of the feeling. It was real. He thought, I don't feel anxious, I feel very calm. He looked up from his desk, and his eyes immediately went to a picture of his family. It was a time in his life when he was genuinely happy. He could feel now what he felt then. He was a sophomore in college and the world seemed kinder to him then. It was before grad school when he was too self-confident for his own good. He became ruthless and cunning. He cared less if he hurt one's feelings. Clint was self-centered and oblivious to the pleading of those that cared for him. He pushed friends away and became judgmental to those who didn't measure up to the high standards he had put on those he came in contact with. He had learned how to use his words to cut like a knife and leave those at the receiving end on their knees.

CHAPTER 19

To Call Or Not To Call

After hanging up the phone, Tanner sat staring into the darkness. He felt confused and did what she did best to prioritize her thoughts. She used to do this on paper when she was in college and began to feel overwhelmed. It was her way of gaining control of her immediate world as far as much as she possibly could. She began with the simplest and worked her way through the characters in this instance. Thinking to herself, "Lexi Girl, she's good. She's always good. There's nothing there to write. Brint?" she pondered. Her thoughts came to an abrupt stop almost as if she had hit a brick wall. Unable to move forward with this thought at the moment, she shook her head as if she were shaking off the water that had just drenched her except it was events instead of water drops. She raised her phone and called Sara.

"Sara, you are going to kill me, I know!" she said with a frantic start. Before she could get another word out, Sara began cutting her off. In a calm monotone voice, she kept repeating, "Calm down, breathe. Tan, just breathe. I know that you have had a lot on you. We weren't expecting this, but we will work through it. The good news is that things will pause for about a week," Sara said.

"Honestly, I just saw where you have been trying to reach me. I have already talked to Lexi and Brint. I know what has happened, well kind of? So, what do you know?" Tanner asked. "Well, first, I know that Clint Winstead called here first thing this morning, have you heard from him?" Sara asked. "NO!" Tanner yelled.

"OK, no big deal. I am sure he was just calling to fill us in on the story. He does represent him. He didn't say anything other than what the television has stated. They found Mr. Copeland dead yesterday morning in his home. They do not know if it was a murder, suicide or natural. The county coroner will be performing an autopsy and will provide details as they come." "I should call Clint," said Tanner. "Do you have his number?" Sara responded. "I do, I figured that you would ask."

"Do you think I could call him tomorrow, or do you think that I should call him now?" Tanner asked. "I think it could wait," said Sara. "Umm, I don't know, I am so worked up. You have no idea," said Tanner. "Then call him, we are an hour earlier then you are," Sara explained. "OK, I think I will. Hey, thank you for looking out for me," said Tanner. "I don't mind, it is my job, but the best job I could have. Good night," said Sara. "Good night," said Tanner.

After she hung up from the multiple phone calls, she finally realized her silence. She loved it. She took in a deep breath contemplating on calling Clint. Did she have it in her tonight or did she just need to deal with it all in the morning? She realized that she just needed to call it a night, and she would cross that bridge in the morning.

CHAPTER 20

Lost Without Her

When the sunlight started to trickle through the window, Brint could feel the warmth on his face. He rolled over and laid there staring at the rays and the different shadows they cast throughout the room. He never noticed this before because he was always up before sunrise. He also realized how quiet it was. There was no smell of shampoo and body wash from the bathroom. There was no scent of coffee brewing. Even Berkeley was nowhere to be found. He felt hungover from the emotions from his conversation with Tanner. He couldn't remember a time when he ever felt this way. They had not fought, yet he felt the pang in his heart as if they had.

He felt very distant from her this morning, and his mind started wondering and analyzing again. He tried to push the thoughts aside and found it very difficult. He rolled over and found her pillow again and took deep breaths. Brint was hoping to find some comfort yet there was none to be found, not today. He threw the covers back and sat up, then deliberately placed his feet on the floor shoulder width apart and began staring out the bedroom window. He didn't have any plans for the day and thought he might walk to the coffee shop down the street instead of making it. That would give him a reason to take a shower and clean up.

As he walked to the shower, it hit him. "When have I ever needed a reason to get up and show up? Never!" he thought to himself. He started the shower; it always took it longer to warm up for the first in line. He brushed his teeth then stepped in the shower. The water stream soaked his face, and he stood there for what seemed like an hour. He leaned further in and allowed the water to hit his shoulder blades, as he placed both hands on the wall in front of him. He could not remember when he felt so weak. His heart felt like it was pounding from the anxious feeling building in his stomach. He reached for the shampoo squirted a blob in his hand, and quickly massaged the soap through his hair. Thinking to himself, "I got to get out of here, I am going to suffocate." The water was hot, but no more than usual. He couldn't dry off quick enough and didn't bother to shave.

He opened the closet and grabbed a t-shirt, a pair of blue jeans, and a pair of Chaco sandals. He almost sprinted to the kitchen, grabbed his keys, and ran down the steps instead of waiting on the elevator. Once he reached the road, he stood beneath a mature maple tree, which had already turned a brilliant yellow and had hints of light green. The leaves rustled in the soft breeze, and he could feel fall in the air. He stood there filling his lungs with as much air as he could. Brint was lost in his thoughts and began to say to himself, "I think I might not make it without her." He had never stopped long enough to appreciate all the things he had come to depend on. Even when she wasn't there, she was there. Why did he feel so distant all of a sudden with no reason at all?

CHAPTER 21

The Call

He put a call in to his secretary. "Hey Merritt, with all that has come down this weekend, the week should be fairly calm not anything that you can't handle or that you can't contact me about. I am going to take some time away," Clint said with a sigh, much-needed time away he thought to himself. "When should we expect you back?" she asked. "Actually, I am not certain. It may be a week, or a couple of weeks. You know what is urgent and what is not. I am taking my computer and will be able to work remotely. I will check in each morning, and if you need me just call," he said. Merritt thought to herself, "He is usually polite and professional. But am I hearing a completely different tone? Is he being sweet?" Shaking the thought from her head, she made a couple of notes and replied, "That sounds good. I will talk to you soon," she said.

"Good evening, Merritt," Clint replied.

After hanging up the phone, Clint headed to his wet bar to

pour himself a drink. Pouring a small amount of Woodford Reserve, one of Kentucky's finest, he raised the glass to his lips and took a small sip. He added a couple cubes of ice and headed to open the balcony doors. He felt relaxed, in control of himself. Clint was feeling confident, but not overly confident. "This is good. This is a glimpse of what I have needed for such a long time," he thought to himself.

As Clint stared out over the city, listening to the sounds, he seemed to be rolling through thought after thought of people he needed to make contact with for one reason or another, because of his actions or words. He thought, "I can keep my edge by doing things ethically and treating people with respect. Treating people as I have for so many years makes me nothing but a bully." He was trying not to beat himself up, however, he couldn't help but feel disappointed with himself.

CHAPTER 22

Remembrance

Just like clockwork, Tanner's eyes fluttered open. She took in a deep breath. She thought to herself, "I must have absolutely crashed. I barely remember my head hitting the pillow." She rolled over staring out the window making a mental note. The lake had always made her feel close to her Savior. It had always been a place that she could feel free to be herself. She always thought that this was as close to heaven on earth that she could be.

She felt like everything that she looked at or smelled was made by her creator. Sometimes she found it mesmerizing to just look at everything individually to specifically take it in and appreciate it with all she had. It made her feel calm and in control. This morning she looked at the individual sparkles that the sun made as it reflected off the water. They were fairly spread out as there was not much movement on the water this morning.

She felt excited to get her day started. Although, with the news from the night before, it was not going to begin as she had originally planned. Her thoughts immediately went to Clint. She actually heard herself groan with a mix of annoyance and a bit of frustration, and it broke the silence and brought her thoughts back to reality. She sat on the edge of the bed for a moment and then sprang to her feet. She made a B line straight to the bathroom.

Tanner turned on the shower as she remembered it always took a bit for it to warm up. She brushed her teeth and washed her face. By the time she finished she was feeling awake. She hopped in the shower, immediately pushing her head under the water. Feeling anxious, she didn't linger long. She jumped out of the shower and wrapped her hair in a towel. Skipping her robe, she immediately put on her water shorts and tank top. She searched for her Chaco sandals and headed to the kitchen.

Coffee was the first thing on her agenda. She opened the cupboard, and sure enough, there was her favorite. Thinking to herself, my mom knows me so well. She started a pot thinking four cups should do it just in case she had company. She thought that her dad or mom might come by this morning.

Tanner popped a bagel in the toaster, she then looked in the refrigerator, her mom had done it again, Philadelphia strawberry cream cheese. She spread a glob on her bagel and followed it by a sip of her coffee.

She took her place at the table in the kitchen. Tanner looked around and for a moment felt a bit lonely. She thought of Brint. She thought about how fast paced their lives were in Chicago and that they never took the time to sit together and have breakfast in the morning. She made a note mentally whether she meant to or not, I don't like that we don't do that. She finished her bagel and took her plate to the sink, washed it off and placed it back inside the cabinet. They didn't have a dishwasher like she did in Chicago. She thought to herself. How simple to not have to deal with loading and unloading. It was a task complete she thought. Simple was something she liked.

Again, another thought popped in her head. Brint had been raised in a very commercialized family. They had a gadget for every-thing and the latest of everything. She remembered that when she visited his parents' house that she was scared to touch anything for fear it would beep at her, talk to her, or begin to move.

They even had a touch screen on their refrigerator. She rolled her eyes to herself, and she took the rest of her coffee and walked toward the back porch. She opened the door and was met by the crispness of a cool September morning breeze. Looking out over the lake, she started to prioritize her day in her mind. I will gather my thoughts and call Clint. Then I can get that in my past and then

I am going to get the kayak out of the shed. I will spend the rest of the morning on the lake. I will paddle over to the island, eat my lunch, and read my book. Her thoughts were interrupted by the sound of her phone. The noise annoyed her. She thought as soon as I can I am silencing that stupid thing. She picked it up and noticed immediately that it was a Chicago number.

Her heart skipped a beat, and she cleared her throat. In the most chipper voice she could find, she pressed the green button and said, "Hello, this is Tanner." There was a brief moment of silence, and then she heard, "Tanner!" The voice on the other line was very familiar. She knew without a doubt who it was.

"Clint!" Followed by another brief moment of silence. Without the skip of a beat, they both started at the same time with, "Hi!" They both kind of chuckled and then again, silence. Tanner's heart felt like it had sped up to marathon pace, her legs suddenly felt like jelly, and she felt lightheaded. All of these feelings suddenly made her mind go completely blank. She found the couch and knew if she didn't sit quickly that she would surely faint.

Finally, gaining her composure, she thought to herself, "Oh heavens, how long have I been silent." Clint started first, "Did I catch you at a bad time?" he asked. Stammering a bit, Tanner began, "Oh, no, I was just out on the porch having my coffee." Hearing the birds in the background, Clint knew exactly where she was and knew approximately where she was standing. It was a very familiar site to him. His mind was racing.

Although, he was such an expert at hiding his thoughts and feelings that Tanner would have never known that he was sitting there with this image burning in his mind. "So, you are at the cabin, I'm guessing," he said. "Yes, I am. How did you know?" she asked. "I can hear the birds in the background, and you said porch." Chicago doesn't have porches and you definitely cannot hear birds in the city," he said with a chuckle.

"You're good, you would almost think that you were an attorney or something," she said with a bit of tease in her tone. "Funny, TJ," he said. Hearing Clint call her TJ, made her blush. Feeling the blood flush her cheeks. "Clint?" Suddenly Clint felt a bit awkward. "Tanner, I am sorry, I should not have called you that. You are a colleague. That was not very professional of me. I apologize," he said. "Don't worry about it, it's OK, really. We have known one another for a very long time. It's not like we don't have a past. Let's just acknowledge it up front and get that out of the way," Tanner responded. "Sure, you are right. So, have you heard?" he asked. "I have, my phone blew up last night. I am sorry to hear about this. It is kind of shocking," she replied. "It is very shocking!" said Clint with an excited tone. "What happened?" Tanner asked.

"They really don't know. It looks like he took his own life, but considering his position in society, they are looking at all scenarios," Clint told her. "Well, I guess I won't get my day in court against you," she said. "So, you were looking forward to it," he responded. "Oh, I was! I was going to get my chance to finally put you in your place," Tanner exclaimed. "Well, it sure didn't take long to bring back those old feelings. You really don't like me, do you?" he asked. "Oh, Clint! I am sorry. That wasn't very professional of me. Can we start again?" she asked apologetically. "Tanner, you don't need to apologize, it is well-deserved. I have a lot I need to apologize for, too," Clint admitted.

Hearing Clint say the word apologize and sorry in less than five minutes was a bit concerning. "Clint are you well?" she asked. "Tanner, I am fine. Actually, I am better than fine," he said. There was another long silence. "Are you there? Tanner?" Clint asked. "Yes, yes, I am here," she said. Tanner was feeling confused to the point she felt dizzy. She imagined that it was probably from the quick adrenaline rush. She found herself taking a moment to collect herself before she continued. This had caught her off guard. She had planned to call him, of course, but after she had mapped out how the conversation was going to go.

"Before we continue, I have a couple of things that I need to share, Clint," she said as she started back the conversation, and he immediately cut her off. "No, I need this time please, we are not in a court room and there are no objections, OK," he said. He heard a sigh, but all he could think for a moment was that one of the sweetest sounds he had heard in a long time. Getting his thoughts back together, he took in a deep breath. "OK, where to start? Tanner, there is a lot I need to say. If you could just feel what is in my heart you would understand, and I would not even have to try to put it into words. You see, I need to, I want to, and I just need you to hear me out. I guess the best place to start is from the beginning," Clint said sweetly.

CHAPTER 23

The Confession

"From the very first time that I met you, you, and everything about you, intrigued me. We were kids, and it wasn't cool to like a girl. So, following what I had seen from my older brothers, I thought giving you a hard time was a way to pay attention to you. Year after year, I would see you at the benefit, and, as we grew older, my feelings for you grew. Then I had no clue how to treat you, because there was always the unspoken competition between our families. I was young and didn't realize that it was a healthy competition. Once I realized that, I thought it was time to tell you.

Unfortunately, I wasn't done growing up yet. As you know, you lived that part, but I have to acknowledge my behavior, or you will never know my sincerity. I know that I did not respect you as you deserved. Those times when I would leave you hanging, not knowing where I was or if I was alive, deep down I knew it was wrong but for some reason my actions did not reflect that. I should have never left you to wonder. I should have never given you reason to doubt me or us. I realize now that I took advantage of your trust, and in every way, made a mockery of the person you were you are. I realize that someone with a pure heart as yours is very rare and I played with it, like a cat plays with a toy. I was wrong," confessed Clint.

Then, Tanner interrupted, "Clint!" "No! T! Not this time! I am not finished, and this is very important! Very! I'm sorry for raising my voice. When I realized that you were the opposing counsel, I felt like all I wanted to do was anything that made you look bad. I laid awake thinking of ways I could get back at you, so to speak, but publicly.

I was humiliated as I should have been when you called me out for the coward, I was in front of my friends that night. I realize now that you had every right. Everything you said was right. It cut deep. I laughed at you with my friends, because I thought that it made me look like the bigger person.

I spent so much time trying to make myself look better than the picture you painted, that I came to believe that I was better than anyone else. I took on that persona in everything I did. With whomever I met, business or personal. It came to provide the confidence I needed to make myself an excellent attorney, but I recently realized that it has not made me a very good person.

The closer the court date got, the more I couldn't sleep. Not because I was laying concerned about the trial, but because I was feeling so competitive that I could not wait to face you in court to show off how good I was and make you feel incompetent. I know, please don't say it. I can't believe my mind could even work this way. It is wrong in every way.

Then, I would fall asleep thinking horrible thoughts and then dream of how amazing I really had it and I ruined it all. It was like I was being shown what life could look like. It was truly genuine. Deep in my soul I know that now. I remember what a sincere heart you had, and I remember how you always put everyone ahead of yourself. I never deserved you. There is absolutely no way in my whole life I could ever make up for my thoughts or my behavior. I hate that Mr. Copeland is no longer here, but maybe this is what it took to bring me back to earth. My head has been reeling since I received the news. So be it.

I have worked for their family since my career began. This does not count the longevity of the relationship that my father had built. I always thought that he had everything and come to find out, he had nothing. I know this is a lot. I'm almost finished, but this is the most important part. The other night," pausing, Clint looked at the ceiling and his eyes filled with tears. The importance of what he was sharing quickly overwhelmed him. He felt such sincerity in his heart. He made a mental note of that feeling in his heart.

"Clint?" Tanner said calmly. "Are you OK? Clint?" she responded. "Yeah, I'm here, just give me a minute," he asked. "Sure," she said. "Take your time." Tanner wasn't sure what was coming next, and as she was feeling a bit overwhelmed from the pouring of emotions. She understood that he was feeling sorry, and she was appreciative for the sincere apology, but there was way more going on than she could wrap her head around she almost felt sorry for Clint.

Reminding herself to stay strong, she waited in the silence. Hearing a sniffle, she began, "Clint, you really don't have to do this. I do understand. I get it. We have a huge past. It wasn't perfect, although I really fell hard. I fell hard for the good, the bad, and the ugly. I loved you" she said confidently clear minded, and genuinely.

Hearing the word loved in past tense had a slight sting to it, Clint thought. "Clint, I meant what I said, I understand," she said. "Tanner you are doing what you always do, trying to make it easier for everyone else. Don't, not now, not ever. I will not stand by and let you do that to yourself any longer! I mean it!" Clint said stern and protective. Tanner noticed she liked his tone. "OK," she said then fell silent. At this point she had no clue what was coming next.

CHAPTER 24

Coffee Shop Talk

Turning in the direction of the local shops, he decided to deliberately walk slowly. Looking at the ground and taking note of the leaves that had already fallen, some were still filled with the colors of fall reds, greens, and yellows and then some that had blended together like a brilliant watercolor painting. He could smell the dampness of the leaves and the crispness of the air mixed with the warmth of the sun. He looked up and the first sight was a mom pushing a stroller and her husband beside her. They were obviously enjoying their morning together. They seemed excited about life. They seemed connected even though they were not sharing words. He thought, will we ever look like that?

Trudging on, he suddenly began to feel like he was walking up an incline although, there were no inclines in Chicago. His heart felt heavy. He quickly shook it off. Thinking to himself, where are these feeling coming from? Answers, I need answers. Reaching the coffee shop, he stepped inside and noticed the girl behind the counter. She was about Tanner's height, had flawless ivory skin, and thick milk chocolate hair that cupped around her face.

Her eyes were a light blue and sparkled as she broke his thoughts. "Welcome to The Coffee Shop, what can I fix for you today?" the young lady asked. "Oh, goodness, um let's do something different. What do you suggest?" he asked. "Do you like flavored coffee?" she asked. Brint shook his head, happily, like a dog begging for a treat. "OK, then how about our Roasted Walnut Vanilla Cream?" she suggested. "Sure, that sounds, wonderful. Very fitting for this time of year," he said. "Yes, it is, and it is one of our best-sellers during the holidays," she added.

Brint reached in his pocket and took out the wad of cash he had grabbed off the dresser and stuffed in his pocket. He laid a five on the counter and waited for his coffee to arrive. Making small talk he asked, "Are you new here, I don't believe I have seen you in here before?" "Yes, I am Maggie's sister. I am just here for Fall break," she said. "Oh, OK, you are the one that goes to interior design school?" Brint asked. "Yes, I decorated this place," she said. With a confident smile on her face, she placed the wide rimmed mug of coffee on the counter. She whisked the five from the counter and opened the register with a ding. Without missing a beat, she finished their transaction, with a flirty, "Thank you." Almost finishing her sentence, "Brint, my name is Brint," he introduced himself. "Brint, it is nice to meet you, I am Kenzie," she said.

As he turns to find a place to sit, she was on to the next customer. Before he was out of earshot, he heard. "That is Brint, the guy I was telling you about. He is marrying my friend Tanner," said Maggie to her sister. Overhearing the sisters whispering to one another, he raised his eyebrow, thinking to himself, "Wow, a topic of conversation we were!" He smiled at the thought.

Brint made his way through the custom-built, wooden tables. Each had a small, white candle flickering inside a medium size, hurricane lamp. There was a stone fireplace directly across from the register with four wheat- colored, oversized chairs facing one another with a large, oversized coffee table in the middle. There were the latest newspapers and magazines scattered across the table. USB plugs were at each chair and cable knit blankets wrapped across the arm of each one. It was truly a place to find your thoughts, or get away from your thoughts, or just relax from life. It seemed to be just what he needed this morning.

The fire was flickering in the fireplace, and it drew him toward one of the chairs. He made himself comfortable crossing one leg over the knee, he began to thumb through the Tribune that he had picked up from the table. He lifted his mug to his lips, smelling a hint of each specific scent, yet, when it touched his pallet, he could mostly taste the vanilla. It was warm all the way to his stomach and made him take in a deep breath, lower his shoulders, and push his anxiety away. He could hear the faint sound of instrumental guitar music as it hummed through the speakers above. It almost was in tune with the flickering flames.

He turned his focus back to the paper and began to browse. Suddenly he felt the urge to call Tanner. He knew she would be awake by now and getting ready for her day. He wondered what was on her agenda. He thought she may go for a run, she may sit on the dock, she may go out in the kayak. He had no clue, but he suddenly wanted to be with her so badly. He quickly flipped the page and settled back on a story that caught his eye: Chicago Crime Rises 32 Percent. Taking another sip of coffee, he began reading what he already knew. It didn't take any thought to get through this article at all.

He began scanning again when he heard that cheerful, confident, beautiful voice behind him. "How is your coffee, would you like a refill? Can I get you one of our famous pieces of Banana Nut Crumble Cake?" she asked. Turning toward the voice, he gathered himself. "You know, I think I might pass on that right now, although it sounds wonderful. Do you always serve that here, I don't remember seeing it on the menu in the past?" asked Brint.

"No, usually I make it when I am in town. It's my specialty they say," she added. "Oh!" Brint said with a peaked interest in his tone. "Well, in that case, I believe I might have a small slice," he said. "Absolutely, coming your way," said Kenzie turning quick with a bounce in her step. Brint made an opinion that either life had not gotten to that girl, or she had a magical ability to push real life aside and completely live in the moment. Either way, she was a breath of fresh air.

When she returned with the cake, she delivered it on a glass plate that had caramel drizzled across the top before the cake was placed on top. It looked like something out of a Southern Living Magazine. He knew because they showed up monthly in their mailbox. Tanner loved browsing through her Southern Living Magazines, especially around this time of year. She would dog ear recipes, stating that she was going to eventually try this recipe or that recipe. He loved watching her excitement as she looked over each picture.

He loved how from time to time she would say, "Hey B, look at this!" It made him feel a part of what she loved. So much of their relationship was hustle, bustle and focused on their work schedules.

Quickly bringing his focus back to the present, he took a small bite. Looking at Kenzie directly this time, he asked. "So where did you learn to bake like this? "He placed the fork back on the plate after savoring the bite completely and maybe a bit too long. "You are a wonderful baker. Are you sure you are not studying for the wrong profession?" he asked. Kenzie chuckled. "I have been asked that a million times. I absolutely love to do both, so I have found a way to incorporate the two. You will find in my portfolio that in every room I design, there is usually a plate of cookies, cake, or fruit displayed in the pictures.

Depending on the project, there are a few dinner specials. I mainly like to bake. I ensure that they include The Coffee Shop website in the article and there, I have a small blog about what I am concocting next. That is where my heart is. I feel like the way a room is designed and how it makes you feel can lead to the type of hunger one may have. Therefore, it all goes together. Before you say anything, I know that sounds silly but it's how my mind works. It just is. I quit trying to figure it out a long time ago. So, I go with it," she confessed.

"You don't have to defend yourself with me. I get it. I think we go with what's easy way too often in lieu of truly pairing what is right," he agreed. In a confirming tone, Kenzie smiled and quickly replied, "Exactly! I think you have to think a little longer and ask yourself a few more questions before coming to a conclusion. That is how I got where I am. I wouldn't change anything for the world.

Enjoy, and I will check on you in a bit," she added. Watching her walk away he suddenly had a thought. A strong thought. He took another bite of his cake, enjoying every morsel as it rolled across his tongue. He followed it with a sip of his coffee, and it was the perfect combination. Just like everything in his current surrounding. It all went together, and all made sense. It was easy.

THE MESSIAH

CHAPTER 25

You Made Me Strong

"Clint, I am going to be honest, dead honest with you. When I met you, I had been just making it by. Taking day by day, feeling like I was living, but I wasn't. I had my vision. I was fairly determined that I was going to make every aspect of it come true. So, determined that there was a lot of signs I missed. All I knew was I felt like we came easy. Our conversations, our adventures, our connections were everything. I had not felt that ever. It wasn't like you were my first relationship, but it was the best I had ever had. We were a little wild, with a little crazy, and then we found our own. Things settled down, and we were on the same page, I thought. I became comfortable, with your family, your friends.

What I didn't like well, I don't think I want to walk down that road. It took me about three years to get over that. However, I have to tell you that without that pain, without each of our amazingly good experiences, the amazingly painful tears, I would not be who I am today. I mean that, and it's a great thing. In fact, I really need to thank you. I would have never learned about what true heartache felt like, and I am thankful for it. I would not have known what true happiness and love felt like, even if it was one sided, and that's OK. I am so very thankful for it all. It took me a bit to sort it out, but once I did, my eyes were wide open. Life was actually just beginning for me. My career started falling in to place. I purchased my first home, I had my vision, and I had everything I wanted. You just weren't in it. You taught me to be tough. You thickened my skin. You taught me about gut instinct. In our profession, it's a must. I know you had no idea you were doing all of this but thank you. You helped make me successful as a person and a professional.

I hate what brought this phone call to reality, but I am so grateful that we are able to get the air cleared. Just like you said you have been having thoughts, I, too, have been having feelings leading up to the trial. It was almost like every emotion one can have rising to the surface. I found myself feeling like I was suffocating. Although, I must add that I was having difficulty figuring out what part was from going up against you and what part was me trying to mentally prepare myself for getting married," Tanner said as if she had just given a closing statement in court.

Clint suddenly felt his heart feel like it was going to stop. He thought to himself, "Married? Did she just say married? How did he not know? Getting married?" "Oh!" Clint said, feeling his eyebrows raise. "Well, I guess I need to tell you congratulations!" he told her as he tried his best to sound sincere, because for the first time in this conversation he wasn't. "Thanks!" she said. "So, when is the big day?" he asked. "Well, I just went for my last dress fitting, and the wedding is in two weeks," she said. Clint was great at reading between the lines, and he was good at putting timelines together. Product of his profession, he guessed. "Tanner, I am not being a smart ass, I mean, maybe I don't need to say this, but I am going to because it is a thought. I am being completely honest and transparent here." So, if we were supposed to go to court in less than a week, and you are trying to get ready for a wedding, what took you to the lake house? I have to know, was it the case. "Did I do that to you?" he asked. Sounding remorseful, Clint placed the questions out there and could not take them back.

"Wow!" said Tanner responding and suddenly sounding a bit annoyed with him. "I'm sorry, I shouldn't have asked. It is absolutely none of my business," he said quickly understanding her tone. "Well, we are being completely transparent and putting it all out there, right?" she admitted. "Yes," he said.

"Then yes, you did do this to me. I am supposed to be getting married and all you have done is make me doubt. Every night, I leave the office feeling stressed, not because of the case, but because I am questioning everything I am doing. Everything! Now, I am sure you are wondering why would you be making me doubt. Well, I will tell you!" said Tanner as her voice began to sound very emotional, and her voice became very stern as if she was about to put the dot's together for the jury. Although, there were no jury present or any witnesses to decide.

"Tanner," said Clint as he cut in, trying his best to not sound callous as he had always been in the past. This was not how he wanted to be described ever again. "Tanner," he said in a more concerned steady voice. "Please hear me out. Please. I really need to take the floor for a moment," he pleaded. "Of course, have at it," she said. Tanner was prepared to hear old Clint, although she was clearly confused, because it was blatantly obvious that something was different.

She decided to calm down a bit. Clint could hear her take a deep breath, and all he could feel was shame. He knew without a doubt that he needed to make this right. It was not for a chance with her, but because Tanner deserved it. He knew, without her understanding and forgiveness, that he would find it extremely difficult to keep from resorting to his old ways. Clint believed that Tanner was his motivation for wanting to become a better person. He believed that she had been placed in his life for a reason. He realized completely that he had messed things up on many levels in earlier years. Shaking his head, closing his eyes, he whispered, "I've changed."

CHAPTER 26

Innocent Feelings

After Brint took the last sip of his coffee, he sat staring into the flames in the fireplace. He sank deeper and deeper into thought. Kenzie looked in his direction and notice that he was at least a thousand miles away. She decided to move on to the next chore instead of walking over to take his plate or offer a refill. She found that she couldn't take her eyes off of him. Finding herself in a trance, she made a mental note of his kind but confident eyes. His hands were bigger than the cup. They were muscular.

His jawline was strong. Must be a family trait she thought.

Just then, Brint looked her direction and obviously caught her staring at him. A slight smile crept across his face, and he then quickly looked back at the fire. She began to tidy the counter behind her. Brint glanced in her direction noticing that she was super busy and chuckled knowing the feeling of getting caught. All of a sudden, he felt the blood rush to his face. His heart was skipping a beat, and all he could think about was what if Tanner were to walk in and catch his stare? He thought, "You stupid idiot you just flirted, and you just enjoyed that conversation a bit too much for a man who is engaged and getting married. You need to stop it!"

Breaking his thoughts, he heard Kenzie's voice, "Hey, are you ready for

a refill?" "Ah, no," said Brint. Sounding a bit startled, he was completely caught off guard. "No, I think I am ready for my check, if you don't mind," he said. "Absolutely, I will be right back," she said. When Kenzie returned, she handed the check to him and smiled, "You can pay up front at the register." He smiled, then looking at his receipt, he noticed that she had circled the total, signed below with a smiley face, and had placed a phone number below. He was smart enough to know that this was not the stores number. He smiled and shook his head. He couldn't help but feel a bit flattered by the gesture. He also thought, this was the first time that a girl had made the first move.

He felt a little self-inflated as he approached the counter. He looked Kenzie eye to eye, handing her the ticket and a twenty-dollar bill. He smiled confidently at her and told her to keep the change. "Thank you! You are too kind. Will I see you again?" she asked. Kenzie was beaming. Brint looked down at the counter and then back at Kenzie. "I really enjoyed our conversation, but I am engaged," he admitted. "Oh!" Kenzie replied in a slightly higher voice than she had anticipated, catching herself off guard. "You know, I should not have put myself out there like that. It was a little assuming. Well, I guess you know what they say about that and here I stand," she confessed.

Laughing at herself, Brint could not help but notice how beautiful she was laughing at herself and thought how relieved he was that she took it so well. "Please come back to see me. I mean us, come back to see us!" she said. "I will, I enjoy the atmosphere," he added. Brint gave Kenzie one last smile and slowly walked out the door. He stopped for a moment, taking a deep breath, and gathered himself. He quickly came to the conclusion that he would not go back in unless he had Tanner with him. Kenzie must meet Tanner.

Standing there, he looked left, and he looked right, and noticed that the streets had become more crowded than they were before. He wondered

where everyone was going and what kind of agenda they had. He wondered what Tanner was doing. He wanted to be with her. He took his phone out of his pocket, flipped to his favorites, and tapped her number. The phone began ringing, but there was no answer. He placed his phone back in his pocket and headed toward town.

The closer he came to the park, the more couples he noticed. Some couples were walking hand in hand, side by side, and some were sitting on blankets having brunch. People were throwing frisbees with their pets or just sat side by side staring at nature. Parents were chasing around their children and runners were in groups. Everyone had their own agenda and their own cadence it seemed. He wondered what couple he and Tanner resembled.

He noticed that there were a few individuals doing the same as the couples, but he felt like he was the only one that looked lost. Brint definitely felt lost. This was not a familiar feeling, and he had absolutely no idea what to do with it or how to channel it. He took out his phone and tried Tanner once more. The phone rang four time before her message came on. It was so good to hear her voice, even if it was only her voice mail. He hung up without leaving a message. With a deep sigh, he wandered toward a vacant bench. Sitting there keeping to himself, trying not to draw attention he became lost in thought.

CHAPTER 27

Coming Clean

Laughing, Tanner blurted out, "That's what everyone says. Seriously, T, just listen," said Clint as he pleaded this time. "No! Clint! You listen. I am not going to sit here and listen to you use your words on me. I have changed too!" argued Tanner. Knowing that he needed to let her get it out, Clint sat quietly. He listened to her words and could feel each of them cut deeply. He knew that every word was true. The recourse he felt was indescribable. "I learned that you used my naivety against me. You took advantage of my heart. You used me physically and mentally. You were the cat, and I was the mouse. I felt like you batted around my feelings like a cat would play with a mouse until it died.

But guess what, I didn't die! I finally figured out how to use my hurt and my anger to make myself a better person. I focused my energy which allowed me to graduate at the top of my class with honors. Thank you! Without you, I may not have been able to achieve that. Then, I spent four years in corporate real estate. That is where I grew my wings and began to fly. Unfortunately, I was forced to grow up even quicker when I was forced out by one of the partners who wanted to bring her best friends' son on board. I was fresh out of the training program and had never worked for a large firm before. I had no idea who I could trust if I decided to trust anyone. You left me without the ability to trust. That was a big one. I navigated my way the best I could without a clue that I was being set up. I was asked to come in early, putting myself at a security risk, but I didn't think I was allowed to say no. You taught me that, too. I was asked to go to meetings that didn't exist. I didn't make a complaint, because I didn't know who to go to. I just kept trying to stand my ground, because I was determined that I was not going to fail.

Guess what, I failed anyway. They called me in one day and told me that I had missed an important meeting, and that I was fired. This really did me in. I had finally got my feet underneath me and then had the rug jerked out from under me again. Luckily, I had the hurt you caused me help push me forward. Thank you again," said Tanner with a sigh.

"Wait, I didn't have anything to do with you losing your job," Clint said. "No, you are right, you didn't. However, because of the way I had been treated by you, I did have the strength to get back up, and dust myself off. I was drawing on my hurt to fuel my fire to do things for me to protect me. I decided that I was never going to let anyone take advantage of my heart or my mind ever again. That is when I went into business for myself. And...in a few short years I found my confidence. Do you hear me? My confidence, no one else, and I found my strength, my strength! I do not depend on anyone else for my happiness. I do not rely on anyone else for anything. I don't need someone else in my life. I do not need anyone to take care of me. I do not need anyone else's money, opinions, or" she continued with her rant.

Before, she could finish, Clint said calmly and gently, "Tanner." He waited to ensure she heard him. She was really on a roll, he thought. The conviction in her voice was deep seeded he could tell. It was like no closing argument he had ever heard, and, if there had been a jury, he would surely be sentenced to life. Clint said again with a bit of a whisper to try to change

the tone of the conversation, "Tanner? Please, please listen. Try to calm down and listen to me." "Do not tell me what to do!" she said. "Tanner, I am not, I would never again. I," Clint paused. He took a deep, quivery breath.

Completely realizing how badly he had acted. Quickly thinking, "No wonder girls hated me. No wonder all of his friends were married and happy, and he was never invited along."

Beginning again, "T, let me just cut to the nuts and bolts of why I called.

Can you please just give me this moment? Then, if you tell me to go away, I will and you will never hear from me again," he said. Hearing him say that all of a sudden made her heart sink. "Wow!" Tanner thought, that was weird. Blinking the tears away that had formed in her eyes, she decided to sit back down on the couch. The wind was rustling quietly through the trees and the air smelled so clean. She took in a deep breath. She pulled the blanket around her and said quietly, "I am sorry, my nerve was touched."

Clint laughed, "Nerve, that was only one nerve? I would hate to see what it sounds like if it were multiple nerves!" Both of them chuckled together. Clint thought to himself, there we go, getting back on track. T, I really like us laughing together. Bear with me, this is truly my first time talking about this. The last couple of months, while preparing for this trial, I have had this indescribable lonely feeling. I have been keenly aware of an emptiness that has been embodying me from head to toe. All the confidence in the world has not been able to conquer this feeling. At first, it was dreams of the past. Pausing a moment, our past Tanner, I blamed it on the case and having to go up against you. Then, I blamed it on the fact that I have read all about your many successes, and I have heard what an amazing attorney you turned out to be. There was a part of me that was a bit intimidated. Part of me was worried that you would get the best of me in court and my insecurities would be exposed.

Then I realized it truly didn't have anything to do with any of these things. Well, I am sure it did a little. Oh, how do I say this? I am just going to say it." Taking a moment to collect his thoughts, Clint began. "I, well I was, this is this is a God thing. I heard God talk to my heart. I felt it. T, the other night I felt this peace, but at the same time I felt all of the horrible things that I have ever said or done all at once. It was a release of pain followed by an over-whelming peace. It was sadness that was followed by peace.

Oh, please tell me I am making some sort of sense. Tanner, I prayed. I prayed hard. I prayed for forgiveness. I think that you and I, against one another in court, was for a reason. No, let me go back further. I believe that our fathers going to school together, our summers together, and even our short-lived relationship worked together to make me who I am today. I believe that everything worked together for the good. How I wish you could feel what I am feeling. I wish you could feel what I felt. Tanner, I am sincerely a changed man. I know that I can't take back all the hurtful things that I have said and done, but, if you can, just try to get to know the real me the new me. Please. I believe that's why I called you first, not just because of what happened with Leonard," said Clint. He felt a huge relief. It felt so good to come clean about his thoughts and feelings and even if Tanner chose not to forgive him, he knew he couldn't blame her. He knew he was in a much better place and swore to himself that he would never turn back to the ugliness he once possessed.

CHAPTER 28

The Dreaded Phone Call

"Well, for once I am speechless. Don't you dare say it! I know you are thinking it. Just don't" Tanner screamed. "I wasn't going to say a thing, honest," said Clint. "Really? I know I talk too much, but it's how the good Lord made me! For that I am grateful," she continued. Pausing, Tanner looked out over the water and began to quickly collect her thoughts. "OK, let me just get my thoughts together."

Taking another moment, she took in a deep breath and began. "So, you said get to know you, the real you. When were you expecting this to happen? I mean we haven't seen each other face to face in several years, talked on the phone, nothing. That is one thought. The other thought is you said relationship, we didn't have a relationship. We dated, and I was the object of our words and actions. Clint, I am going to be really honest with you. I really don't know where you are going with this. Wait. I'm talking like I am talking to the old Clint, I'm sorry," she said.

Calming herself and breathing deep, she quickly said a prayer to herself. "My dear Lord, please guide my words. Please don't let me ramble. Please let me say exactly what I want and with the best, purist intentions. Amen," she prayed. "Helloo? Tanner, are you praying?" Clint asked. "I am, I was," she answered. Trying her best not to sound flustered, annoyed, mad, or hurt

she began. "Please just talk to me, the new me. I'm not going to make fun of anything you say. I currently do not have a sarcastic, condescending word in my vocabulary," he explained.

"Clint, I am going to be very honest with you like I said. This call has taken me by surprise, and I really don't know where to begin. So here it goes. I first want to tell you that I'm so very happy for you, and I do believe that our Savior uses people, situations, circumstances, and various other ways to bring us back to Him. I know that's how my faith grew. I have always been a believer and tried to make good decisions.

Staying true to myself has always been my main objective. So, I have to say thank you. Thank you because, without our time together, I may not have grown in my faith. Your heartless words cut me to the bone that night. I had never been more honest and purer with someone in my life. I remember thinking that I always wanted to stay true to myself and refused to change who I was to please someone else. I knew with my whole heart that I loved you in the deepest sense that I knew existed. I had no doubt at all about what I wanted, and I felt like I had shown my most sincere commitment to us. I remember thinking how important trust and honor would be and how it would be part of the cornerstone of our rela-tionship if we were meant to be. I knew when you went to school that it was going to be different. I knew it was not going to be easy.

I was willing, with all that I was, to give it all that it needed to be successful. I prayed and prayed. I have gone through every emotion that is defined since that night. It took me much-needed time to sort through. I have, I am, I mean I have. My faith grew because of you, and I would not trade one tear. I would not trade one sleepless night. I would not trade one lonely evening. I know the love my God has for me and I for Him. He knows my heart and I know that; without Him I am nothing. I know that I would not have made it through your heartache if it were not for my faith in my Father in Heaven. He had a plan, and you were part of it. The good, the

bad, and the ugly hurt. I would do it all again if I knew that it was going to make the person who I am and bring me to where I am today. Clint, with that said, I pray that He will lead you to exactly where you are meant to be. Do not lose this feeling that you have. Fuel it. Put Him first in everything you do. I don't know why the road has led us here. I came to the cabin to sort through my feel-ings and to be close to my God. I wanted to be in His creation and listen for His voice to guide me in this case.

In this case in which I was going to be going up against you, I knew I

didn't want the negative feeling to arise. I wanted to remain professional and represent my client to the best of my ability and for it to come from the best place of me. I also needed to find some calm before my wedding. There, you have it in a nutshell. There was a lot in between the lines, but at the end of the day, I sincerely wish the absolute best for you. I am confident enough in myself and where I am that I can say, I forgive you. I believe my prayers have been answered, and it means a lot that you would share the first steps of your journey with me," Tanner finished with a sigh of relief.

Looking at the phone as it began to vibrate again, she knew that she needed to hang up with the man that broke her heart and give her attention, full attention, to the man that had helped put it back together. "Clint, I have to answer this call, It's Brint. He's called a couple of times now and I need to go," she explained. "Brint, that's his name?" he asked. "Yes," she answered. "Tanner, I hope this is not our last" he tried to respond to her speech. Cutting him off, "Thank you, Clint for calling and it really was good to talk to you. I wish you the best," she finalized her call with him. Without giving him a chance to reply, he heard the dial tone. He sat staring feeling a tug in his heart as it burned a little within him. He sighed thinking he deserved it, and he decided to embrace it for the time being.

CHAPTER 29

Lynn's Reassurance

"Tan!" Brint exclaimed. "Hey!" Tanner was relieved to hear his voice. He had no clue just how relived she was. Oddly, Brint was just as relieved, but Tanner had no idea of his relief. "I have been calling, you and you didn't answer. I tried not to call, but I just had to. I know you wanted peace and quiet," he explained. "Well, I have hardly had peace and quiet since I got out of the shower last night," she admitted. Sighing slightly, "I wish I could have enjoyed that moment a bit longer. So, my plan is to now go to the shed, find the kayak, and go out for a paddle over to the island.

What are you getting into this afternoon?" she asked him.

Trying to keep the conversation light, she found herself feeling jittery. A little confused by the feeling, she did her best to push it back to wherever it had come from. "Well, I went for coffee this morning, by myself I didn't like it. I walked to the park by myself. I didn't like it. I am sitting on a lonely park bench solo, and I don't like it. That is what I am doing. As far as this afternoon? I have no clue what to do and I don't like it!" he cried out a bit louder with each exclamation. Tanner was sensing his frustration. She wasn't sure if this was a side of Brint she had seen before. "I'm sorry. Why don't you go for a run?" she suggested. "I did that yesterday," still raising his voice. "And I didn't like it!" Tanner finished his sentence. They laughed.

"OK, here's the deal. I won't be gone long, and, when I get home, time is going to fly. The next thing you know we will be married, and we are going to love it!" she expressed to him. Brint could see the smile on her face just by hearing the sound in her voice. "You are right. So, I guess I will go for a short walk along the loop and then head back to work a little. Maybe I can get some things caught up, so I don't get too far behind while we are gone," he said with a confident tone. "That sounds like a great idea," she said, but she paused to add before hanging up. "B, I love you with all of my heart," Tanner said with tears in her eyes. "T, you hold mine in your hand, be gentle," he reminded her. "I promise," she assured him.

While Tanner would have rather been out on the lake the very first thing in the morning, she was thankful at this point to be getting out on the lake at all. She had learned over time that she had to be thankful for the short periods of time that were peaceful. She had learned to smell the air and listen to the birds even in the midst of the busiest street. She always made it a point to focus on the most precious gifts in life. Those made by her Creator.

In doing so today, she noticed that someone must have just mowed their yard. One of her favorite scents. There was a slight breeze blowing. The birds were chirping back and forth to one another. They were obviously carrying on their own conversation. She thought to herself how fun it would be if she knew what they were so happy about. She then smiled because it was a corny thought, but that was her. As she pushed the door of her father's shed, it opened. The musty smell of the wood brought back memories of her father using the trees on the property to build the shed. She remembered how he would tell her how to make each cut as he would saw through another piece of oak. He laid each piece out and knew exactly where it would go. He was very methodical about the process. He shared stories about helping his father when he was little.

She remembered her grandfather and how much she loved and missed him dearly. Staring through the doorway, she was suddenly a bit overwhelmed with the feelings building in her chest as she remembered how special her grandfather was. She began to reminisce memories of her dad and grandfather fishing together and sitting at the kitchen table discussing the world's issues. She remembered thinking that there was no one smarter than her grandfather and how much her dad reminded her of him. Tanner realized she had been blessed with an amazing childhood. Taking a few more steps inside, she reached for her red kayak. She remembered picking it out and how the color made her feel happy. She pulled it down and turned to head toward the lake.

She paused a moment to acknowledge the stillness of the water. She was thankful that her grandparents had picked what she thought was the most perfect spot on the lake. It was tucked away from the main channel and the only boats that visited were the owners of the surrounding lots. As she sauntered toward the peer, she made notice of several trees turning to beautiful Fall colors. Some of them were beginning to lose leaves as the breeze blew through them.

She stopped short of the peer making a mental note of the masterpiece before her. She wondered if this was the same perfect image that was seen by her grandmother and by her grandfather when they chose this location. Tanner wondered if the breeze smelled the same to her grandparents as it did to her at this moment. It was a crisp, defined smell of nature, and the fresh cut lawn was comforting to her. It brought back memories of a secure childhood. It was this feeling that she was seeking when she set out yesterday. She just stood there yearning for this feeling to never end. She heard rustling behind her, and it brought her back to reality quickly.

As she quickly turned around, she noticed the neighbors Retriever running toward her. Abby was about ten years old with the energy of a two- year-old. "Abby!" Tanner exclaimed. Abby was excited to see Tanner, and, upon reaching her, she immediately stopped and dropped her ball at her feet. Tanner bent to pick it up and heaved it toward the lake. Abby took off like a bolt of lightning. Looking back toward the house, she noticed their neighbor standing at the top of the driveway. Lynn was a super sweet lady who had moved next door about twenty years ago. She was a young lady then, and she had just lost her husband to a sudden massive heart attack at age forty-three. It had left her lonely with and an entire life ahead of her.

She was forty-one when they had purchased their lot the

summer before and began building immediately. This was their weekend home to come to after a busy stressful week in Knoxville. Her husband was a stockbroker, and the ups and downs of the market kept him on his toes. She was the President of a local community bank which allowed her to be a part of building a beautiful community. She loved her job and served her community through its many development boards which were focused around creating family friendly parks and beautification projects. Lynn was a supportive wife, attending any functions that would allow her husband to meet and greet with his clients and build his client base. She had been honored to stand beside her husband on so many occasions over the past twenty years. They never had any children which was why she was so drawn to Tanner and her sister.

Tanner remembered how much she loved going over to Lynn and Tom's to eat the special desserts that Lynn would bake on the weekends. Tom loved to piddle with her grandfather and father. She remembered all the ladies gathered on the back porch sipping tea and laughing, as the men piddled with this and that and made fun of how they would move from one tiny project to another. They would stand around and talk, looking as if they were about to solve the world's problems in the next moment. Before the ladies could comprehend just what was up, it seemed they were on to the next task.

This seemed to be a ritual that was enjoyed. The ladies were never consulted until one of them would decide they were hungry and would head toward the house to inquire about dinner. There were many nights that Tanner's grandmother, Nell, and her mom would begin rummaging throughout the kitchen and Lynn would bring over leftovers and goods from her kitchen. Together, the women would deliver a delicious meal, complete with scrumptious desserts. They usually consisted of some sort of fish that had been recently caught. Her grandmother would use Mel's special blend of corn meal and other secret spices, that he only shared with one other person (his son-in-law) to season the fish. Mel and Spencer were best friends from the day they met. It sometimes maddened Nell and Madilynn. There were too many nights of the men coming home acting like young boys, rather than mature adults, after a day of fishing.

Lynn waved at Tanner and yelled, "Hey sweet girl! When did you get here?" "Yesterday!" Tanner yelled back. "Are you ready for your big day," Lynn asked, and of course she was one of the first on her guest list. She had sent the most beautiful set of place mats. They were the essence of southern charm with coordinating napkins. Lynn had a great sense of simple, southern charm and knew Tanner's taste to a tee.

Maybe because she had been around Tanner so much and had watched her bloom into the beautiful young lady she was today. "AAAh, I think so. I just went to my last dress fitting before I headed this way," Tanner replied. "I can't wait to see you in it. I know you will look exquisite!" she said.

"Ummm, yeah, I hope so," Tanner answered her. Lynn could since a tone in Tanner's voice that sounded a little uncertain. "I am sure you have a lot on your mind in these final days. It will all come together perfectly and probably better than you imagined," Lynn assured her. "I definitely have a lot on my mind these days, that is certain," Tanner said.

She remembered having so much fun planning her own wedding and how she could not wait for Tom to see her in her dress. She could not wait to be Mrs. Thomas Martin. She smiled as the thought passed through her mind. Lynn yelled back, "Just take it one day at a time." "I will, I am!" she yelled back. "If you need anything while you are here, give me a buzz. I will be here through next weekend. I am taking some vacation time myself," Lynn said. "I will!" Tanner assured her. "Love you sweet girl!" Lynn told her. "I love you too Lynn!" Tanner told her back.

Tanner began her journey toward the lake. She was not even noticed by Abby as she ran past, kicking up leaves behind her, toward her mamma.

Lynn had begun yelling for Abby as soon as they had ended their chat. Reaching the end of the dock, she lowered her kayak into the water. She sat on the edge of the dock and placed her feet on the top of the kayak to hold it in place.

Getting Ready For A Trip

As Clint hung up the phone, he felt a peaceful sadness. He sat staring for a moment. He realized that he had just tackled something that had been on his mind so heavily. He felt lighter and healthier. There was so much more, but he couldn't match the words to his feelings. He knew he had done the right thing. He felt free. Feeling the need to focus his energy on something healthy, healing, and raw, he looked over at the Cannondale leaned against the wall. He used to love to ride. He quickly made note that he and Tanner used to love to ride. It was one thing they enjoyed doing together.

He paused, remembering the first time they had ridden together. He invited her to a nearby park. It was not a beginner trail, and he knew she had just begun riding trails. He remembered thinking this would be a good test to see how tough she was. It saddens him to think that this was the objective of his day, not to enjoy her company, to strictly to outdo her. He remembered unloading her bike, looking at her, and laughing to himself. He wanted to pick the phone back up and apologize for that specific moment.

He felt his heart being squeezed by emotion. He felt like he couldn't breathe for a second. He dropped his head and said out loud, "Lord please

forgive me." Standing quickly to refocus, his thoughts began swirling. Thinking to himself, "I can't sit here, I can't stay still, I have to go. Where will I go?" He suddenly got a mischievous idea. He looked at his closet, he looked at his dresser and knew exactly what he wanted to do. Clint pulled his navy-blue Mountain Hardware duffel bag from the top shelf of his closet. He batted the dust off of it, which made him squish his nose from side to side. Blinking, he thought dust should never again collect on my travel agenda. He plopped it on the bed and headed to the bathroom. He threw together his bare necessities for good hygiene and placed them in the bag. A couple pair of gym shorts from his dresser should, do along with a couple pair of dress shorts.

He walked back to his closet, sliding the hangers back and forth, he chose a couple of ratty t-shirts, a couple of polos shirts, and a pair of blue jeans. He grabbed flip-flops, tennis shoes, and his Cole Haan loafers. He then went back and yanked a light blue casual button down off a hanger. He looked at the tag. It read no iron, "Perfect!" he exclaimed. Shaking his head and chuckling at himself, he pulled a pair of pajama bottoms from the bottom dresser drawer and placed them in the bag. Heading toward the front door, he turned around, noticed the dishes, and unmade bed and thought, "I don't care, I am going." Throwing his bag over his shoulder and grabbing his bike handlebars, he picked up the bag with his bike gear in it, and he was on his way. He watched the numbers tick by, 8, 7, 6, 5, 4, 3, 2, 1. Ding, he heard, and the doors slid open. He decided to take his black, Jeep Wrangler Rubicon 4WD. He had modified the tires to handle ugly terrain just last winter. He loved to play in the snow and find places to go off-road. Loading his bike on the rack he paused a moment, and a crazy thought came rushing back. Pushing it back momentarily, he was suddenly hit with another emotional memory.

One of the last dates that he and Tanner had been on had started out sweet. He had picked her up at her apartment in his silver, convertible

BMW 328I. It had been his high school graduation present. He remembered thinking that he was so cool in that car. All the girls had gathered around when he pulled in the school parking lot at graduation rehearsal. They all wanted a ride. He never took interest in them, but he liked having pretty girls around at all times. He was always flirting and carrying on.

As Tanner got into his car, she looked so classy. She was hot in a subtle way. It was a challenge, and he loved a good challenge. After arriving at the restaurant, things had taken a turn for the worse he remembered. He noticed that Tanner didn't seem engaged in their dinner. He had ordered the most expensive wine. Not because she liked it, or because it was her favorite, but because it was just another way to show out. He was annoyed by the way she didn't act impressed. He was annoyed by the way she seemed too independent. He had made note of it when he asked her what she was going to order, so he could order for her, and she never gave him a definite answer.

The conversation between the two of them was one sided, while she sat politely listening. He remembered how she would look down when he would laugh at his own jokes. He remembered how he wanted to grab her chin and make her realize that he was her focus. Clint remembered thinking that he was the only person she should be focused on. He remembered the feeling of rage that was building in him the more she acted indifferent to him. What he didn't know then was he had shattered her dream of being in love. He had snuffed it out like a candle at the end of its time.

Talking to himself as he tightened the straps around his bike, "What an absolute jerk! I could think of a worse description of words which aren't appropriate to say now, and to think last week those words would have rolled right off my tongue." His thoughts continued. He was a bit surprised at how his reactions were changing. However, the ugly memories he was experiencing were physically making him feel sick at his stomach. He wanted to erase them from his memory forever. Knowing it was impossible,

all he could think was "when I find her, I am going to cherish her and make sure she never has a doubt about the love and admiration that is held for her. I will never go one day without putting God and her first. Never!" he said. He felt his phone buzzing but kept on working.

He slid the top back about halfway, climbed in, and cranked the radio. Mötley Crüe's Kickstart My Heart blared to life, and he quickly turned it down. He hadn't driven his jeep in over a month. He tried to remember the mood he had been in then. Honestly, it didn't matter, he was in a mood now and one that he never wanted to end.

CHAPTER 31

Just Lakin'

Looking down at the water, Tanner made a mental note of how clear the water actually was even though as she looked out over the cove it was a deep green. She stuck her foot in the water to get a feel for it. It felt cool and crisp. She drew in a deep breath filling her lungs with the fresh air surrounding her. She thought to herself that she could sit here forever. It was a cleansing feeling. Before she knew it, she was in a deep thought. Just hearing Clint's voice had made so many memories rush back to her. She could always remember the best instead of the bad about their relationship.

Of course, that was the way she was about everything. She remembered one day when they had taken her dad's pontoon boat out and spent the day together. Clint had packed sandwiches and fruit. His mom had made some fruit dip that had a hint of Amaretto. It was amazing she remembered. She could almost taste it now as she ran her tongue across her lips. She reflected how they walked hand in hand down the lush, green grass to the dock. Her dad was yelling behind them to be back before dark. She untied the last rope and Clint started the engine. She remembered thinking to herself that day, "Can he drive a boat, he's never been around a boat." Sure enough, he knew what he was doing.

He always seemed to know what he was doing. Nothing ever seemed new to him. He seemed to be novice at everything. This impressed her. As they headed out to the main channel, she sat at the front of the boat feeling the breeze blow through her hair. She could hear the sounds of Jimmy Buffet coming through the speakers. She looked out across the lake, as the sun danced off the tiny waves, and it looked like diamonds. The trees were a deep green and full of leaves. Everything seemed like it was alive to its fullest, including her.

After finding a perfect spot to anchor, they sat in the silence for a moment. She could hear the water slightly splashing against the pontoons. It was a relaxing sound, and one that she found comforting. She remembered how Clint came up behind her, he placed his left hand on her shoulder, giving her a gentle squeeze and the other one embraced her cheek and chin. He slowly pulled her head back and placed a kiss on her forehead. It was such a sweet gesture that she could feel her heart swell. She stood to face him, and he cupped her face gently and placed yet another gentle kiss on her lips.

They walked to the back of the boat and began unpacking their lunch. He had made tomato and cucumber sandwiches which were her favorite. He had cut up fresh fruit, cantaloupe, strawberries, watermelon, pineapple, and grapes. He had grabbed the jar of sweet tea from her mother's refrigerator and helped himself to the ice in the ice maker for their cooler. She remembered how comfortable he seemed in her mother's kitchen and how he teased with her mother. She loved the way the two of them would bat back and forth with each other playfully. It was comfortable and that made her feel amazing. It was everything she had ever dreamed of.

After eating, they went to the bow of the boat where they placed their towels and sat side by side. She was in love with the fact they could say something or nothing, and it was so fulfilling. She loved the way Clint would reach over and grab her hand and stroke the top of it with his thumb.

Tanner loved that when she would lay her head on his shoulder it was a strong place to rest. He felt confident, sturdy, and safe. The summer had been a fairy tale. They spent many days on the lake, and she remembered that she never wanted it to come to an end. Tanner had fallen in love. Her heart felt full. She imagined how they would finish school and dreamed about getting married. She had imagined this scene her whole life but never knew who with. Now, she seemed to have the complete picture.

She remembered the day that she finally gave in to him. It was magical. He was so considerate, tender, and patient. She knew that she was not his first, and it didn't matter. Again, he knew exactly what he was doing, and she felt confident that following his lead would land them in complete ecstasy. And it did. They stared into each other's eyes. Neither of them exchanged a word, and they didn't have to. It was like they could read what the other one was thinking. Yet another perk of their relationship. She knew, without a doubt, that this was it.

Feeling Abby (the neighbor's dog) stick her cold nose on her shoulder, she jumped back into reality. She realized that she had no clue how long she had been sitting there. Part of her enjoyed reliving that memory. She could feel her heart tighten at the memory with a tinge of longing to relive it again. Shaking it off, because she began to feel suffocated again, she swung her foot in the water because she thought would help bring her back into the now. She used her toes to pull the kayak closer to her. Steadying it with her other foot, she buckled her life jacket and climbed in with one smooth motion. Abby watched intently and then quickly turned to run up the hill.

CHAPTER 32

Brint's Love

Brint was so relieved and happy to hear Tanner's voice that it almost satisfied his every need for the moment. He decided to walk back to the apartment and make a list of everything they were going to need for the honeymoon. He was the master of lists. He always had a yellow legal pad filled with notes about this case or that case! It kept his mind on track and made sure he wasn't missing anything. His buddies at work made fun of him. Yellow legal pads were a bit outdated!

He sat down at the desk in the living room and pulled out the file cabinet drawer. He pulled out a legal pad and found his favorite pen. He was such a creature of habit. He was a consistent personality. No matter what crisis popped up he generally reacted to it the same way. Part of it was the training he had received to not show emotion during certain situations, while he believed part was just how God had made him. He was confident in himself and kept a tight regiment, right down to his exercise and vitamins. Anyone who knew Brint was never surprised by his mood. He was always happy, and if something had him bothered it wasn't usually evident unless you knew him really well.

He was in love with the fact that Tanner had come to know him that well. It was so comforting knowing that she just knew, and he didn't have to explain! She never made more of it than what it was and was there if he needed her! He was in love with knowing that she always had his back. On more than one occasion she had his back even when she strongly disagreed with him. He was in love with their ability to agree to disagree and this challenged him and made him respect her that much more!

She was a woman who knew exactly what she wanted. She was timeless, never following the trends that seemed to change personalities temporarily these days! The girls he had met in the past always seemed to be able to change their personalities to fit the current situation or trend. He remembered thinking how miserable it was to date. You never knew who you were going to pick up and didn't dare bet if that was going to be the same one you took home.

Putting all of these thoughts into perspective made him even more confident about the journey he was about to take with Tanner. He had waited his whole life to find someone like her. He remembered praying for her. He physically and orally prayed for her! He always thought that he would find a girl in college. He wanted one that didn't have any scars. No dramatic past preferably! White as snow. The more time passed the more it became evident that maybe this was not in God's plan for him. Things began to happen in his life that he now feels were preparing him specifically for someone very special. He had come to understand and accept the fact that she may not be flawless.

CHAPTER 33
Clint Remembers

As Clint found a comfortable speed on I-94 westbound, he felt relaxed. The wind was blowing through his hair. He had found a play list on his phone that was travel appropriate. He was suddenly happy that he had upgraded the sound system. Thinking to himself, that factory doesn't do any justice. He normally would have cued up something suspicious, something cutting edge. This was the music that got his blood pumping and put him in the mood to go win no matter what the cost, but not today. He realized that he didn't care about winning. He didn't care about beating anyone down. He wanted to feel free. After talking to Tanner, he realized she was still the same beautiful soul that he had always known. He remembered a time he could have cared less if she even had a soul. That made him feel sad. He decided he would never again treat someone like he treated her.

Clint decided to turn on XM radio, and the song playing was

written about Tanner (Dan & Shay's Nothin' Like You). Yep, this has to have been written about her. "I remember when I first met you...You were twirling your hair... Dancing when there ain't no music...you're the right kind of crazy...you're a light in the dark... I love the way you kiss me...in

front of everybody...there's something 'bout you." Singing every word and picturing Tanner in every line, he felt euphoric. Clint thought to himself how weird it was that you could be driving down the road at 75 mph and have a whole video play through your mind, and yet he was keeping it in the lines. The brain is a complex thing. The next song came on and again, it was like it was reading his mind and his emotions. He kept driving, and he changed stations, He found the next song, and he about had to pull over. He remembered singing this song as he was trying to justify his actions somehow. He liked her at the time, maybe even loved her, he thought. He wanted it to be something insignificant. Clint knew that there was a deeper meaning to their romance, but he refused to let himself go there and why he wouldn't he doesn't know or understand to this day.

The piano played and the music became real. He mumbled the words to himself. He remembered when he first saw her in the bar. He had never seen her outside of the charity stuff their parents were involved in. He remembered she was laughing and throwing a shot back as she high fived his friends. Her hair was curled down her back. It was the color of whiskey. She wore a pair of blue jeans, a light-yellow button up polo shirt and a pair of Keds with no socks. All American, all 90's, she was back then. He remembers catching her eye and looking away. Trying to make it look like he was involved with the pool game going on he turned his back. After he took a shot, she tapped him on the back. They exchanged pleasantries and went back to their friends. He remembered one of his buddies asking who she was and him replying, "Just a girl."

I was a bad man. He then clarified to himself, not bad as in evil, I just didn't care about other's feelings. I was selfish, yeah selfish would be a good description. Drifting in and out of thought. He wanted no strings and that is when his demeanor changed. He remembers the good, the wonderful good and then turning it ugly. Was it because he was afraid to be vulnerable? Maybe? Was it because he knew he had big things in store and

wanted no one or nothing to be in his way?

He turned the radio off and just drove. He picked his speed up a bit and just stared at the white lines passing him. Clint was almost in a trance thinking about the time that they had stayed on the phone for hours right before they had both headed to college. The summer had come to an end, and she was at her parent's lake house for the weekend, and he had gone home to Chicago.

They were tucked in bed hundreds of miles apart, yet they found a way to be together. They used to tell stories to one another. He would start by saying, "Once upon a time there was a beautiful girl that lived down the road," Clint started the storytelling. She would begin her part saying something like, "And she would walk down the dusty road to the open field." "And in the open field was a house, an old two-story white house," he said.

"When she would reach the house, she looked out over the field to see a man walking toward her. He ran toward her," Tanner said happily. "And when he reached her, he would grab her up in his arms and swing her around," he said. "She would giggle and wrap her arms around his neck and her legs around his waist," she said. "And he would kiss her deeply," Clint finished the story. She loved his stories and he loved hers. It was what they did to feel close. He remembered her imagination running wild, and it would sometimes leave him feeling breathless. They would whisper good night and sometimes they would fall asleep listening to each other breathe on the other line. He remembered thinking it was so sweet, and he never did this with anyone else. This was theirs.

The GPS completely interrupted his thoughts! He was happy to be able to finally remember something they had shared that wasn't a reflection of his darker side. He assumed that it was a part of a lesson he was long overdue to learn. His heart skipped a beat with a spike of adrenaline just thinking about what her memories of him are. He imagined that they were probably horrific remembering how their relationship had come to an end.

When he called, it never crossed his mind that she would be anything but polite to him. That was just who she was. It's a miracle she took the call at all!

CHAPTER 34

Tanner Remembers

Tanner grabbed her paddle from the dock and pushed off. The breeze was still blowing, and she could feel it across her skin. It cut through the warm feeling from the intense September sun. It was the perfect day. She looked to the sky and the few clouds that were above were moving slowly. She looked across the lake to the island and began her journey. Each time she placed her paddle in the smooth water breaking its perfection, she could feel the resistance and loved the feeling of her muscles tightening to propel her across the water.

She loved the ripples of her paddle cutting the water and with each stroke she felt invigorated. Once she reached the island, it was a bit shadier than the other side of the lake. The water was almost black. She paused herself, as she filled her lungs with the fresh air. That was one of the reasons she loved this lake. It was spring fed, so it was a bit cooler that other lakes in the area. Because of this the water was clearer and did not have that ugly orange tint to it. She found herself thinking about Brint.

She wondered what he was doing. They liked to kayak together. They liked to take small hikes and camp under the stars. She was so thankful to have found him. He had a way of taking her mind off the things that stressed her, and he always found a way of making he feel safe. For that she was thankful. However, she knew deep down that there was something missing. As perfect as he was, there was something missing.

There was a sense of adventure that was not present. When they would head out on journey's, they were carefully planned out and always knew what time they were leaving and what time they would return. They always knew what route they were taking right down to the last mile. They always knew where they would end up and what they would do while they were there. This partly made her feel safe, but there was a part that made it feel uneventful. It was always a thrill when they would discuss the idea, but it was almost as if the adventure had already occurred once they had finished packing.

Remembering the time that her phone rang one night, Tanner flashed back to when she was sitting on her couch folding clothes and watching TV. It was Clint. He told her that he was coming to get her, and she needed to put on some blue jeans and a long sleeve shirt. She remembered asking where they were going, and he wouldn't tell her. She did as he had requested and patiently waited. Her heart was pounding with excitement to see him just as much as it was pounding with the excitement of whatever adventure awaited.

He arrived promptly, and they were off. He had brought his black, Toyota truck the one that they always took when things might get a bit dirty. The sight of the truck made her heart pound a bit more. She looked in the back and saw a backpack. She just could not imagine. Her mind was whirling. She remembered when she asked where they were going, he just said you are going to love it.

They were heading further and further away from the city lights, and she remembered how dark it was getting. She saw a sign that said Radnor Lake. She had heard of it, but she didn't know much beyond the name. While it seemed like they had driven much further, it had really only been about fifteen or twenty minutes. Once they pulled in, Clint jumped out of the truck and ran around to her side. He pulled the door open with excitement. She hopped out and looked at him quizzically. "Where are we going?" "You'll see," he said. Taking her hand and pulling her along. By the light of the moon, she could tell that they were on a trail. She could feel the rocks under her feet that were semi-buried in mud and mulch from decayed trees. She could smell the dampness in the air and could tell that they were near water.

After walking about a mile, they rounded a corner, and she could see the moon shining down on the water. She could hear the breeze through the trees and the many sounds of nature. In the distance, she could hear an owl hoot. It was exhilarating. She stood beside Clint staring out over the darkness. The water looked black, and the light of the moon shimmered across it like a giant spotlight. It was almost as if they were the only ones on stage in the spotlight, and, because it was so bright, they could not see the crowd before them. They were all alone.

Clint placed a blanket on the ground and sat with his knees pulled to his chest. Tanner looked back, and she could see his hair was slightly blowing in the breeze. Kneeling beside him she said, "This is beautiful. Thank you for showing me such an amazing scene." He didn't reply to her. He just reached toward her with one hand and pulled her to him. As their lips began to touch, he leaned back on the blanket pulling her with him. He wrapped his other arm around her pulling her tight. She could feel the warmth of his breath on her neck. She remembered feeling her heart feel like it was getting gentle electrical shocks.

Sighing as he gently squeezed her, he rolled her over and slowly placed her head on the blanket, his hand behind her head to cushion the contact. He brushed her hair away from her face. As he laid himself beside her, propping himself up on his elbow, he stared deep into her eyes. Out of the silence he whispered, "I think I am falling in like with you." She responded, "Like?" "Yeah, I Like you I like you a lot." She was a bit disappointed, but she also knew that love was a very strong word.

Before she could say anything else, he leaned down and kissed her. She knew she should not do this. This was dangerous and irresponsible. Her parents would be so upset if they knew. She also remembered that she temporarily didn't care about those things. She just wanted him, all of him. She remembered him pulling away and looking at her. He never said a word, but she knew he had figured out that this was somewhere she had never been before.

He kissed her forehead over and over and then whispered in her ear, "I promise I will never hurt you. I promise I will always protect you," he said. She could feel her body become warm with excitement. She knew she shouldn't, but her body was saying she should. It was like a war was going on inside of her. He then pulled her into his arms and held her tight. "I hadn't planned this. I swear! All I wanted was to spend some quiet time here with you. I am sorry." She remembered placing her hand on his as he stroked her face. She looked into his eyes without hesitation and said, "I know." He rolled on to his back, placing one hand behind his head and one arm under Tanner, he stared at the stars and laid in silence. Tanner wrapped her arm over his chest playing with the zipper on his sweatshirt. Flicking it back and forth, she remembered feeling safe, secure, and happy with her decision at the time.

Tanner was jolted back to reality when she heard the motor of a small johnboat nearby. She dipped her hands in the cool water and splashed her face. Just then she realized that she was a bit aroused and was breathing a bit harder than she had been. Thinking to herself, "Why on earth are these memories coming back to me so vividly? I should not be thinking of these things. I am getting married. Married!" she said out loud and then suddenly felt sad. She was sad, confused, mad there was a feeling of shame mixed with a complete variety of emotions. "I am marrying Brint." She thought to herself, that she would never be able to give him all of herself. She was quickly reminded how she gave a part of herself to someone so undeserving after nothing more than flattery.

She knew now more than ever that Brint was her guy. Suddenly, she thought if she could be in his arms, it would erase these memories and make things right. It would put her back in her safe space. Safe space, which is what Brint was. He had never said anything hurtful to her. All he had ever done was treat her like a queen and put her on a pedestal. He took care of her when she needed and was there at all the right times.

She also remembered the night he asked her to marry him. She remembered how caring he was when she worked up the courage to share with him that he would never be able to have all of her. Tanner remembered thinking that he would be so disappointed, and she was fully prepared to give the ring back. He looked at her and simply replied, "But I have you now. We will belong to each other forever. I know who you are, and I know your heart. That is all I want is your heart. May I, have it? Please."

Thinking if she had known then what she knew and understood now, she would have never allowed herself to have gone there. She knew she was with the one God had intended for her life, and she answered, "Yes!" Brint took her into his arms and just held her. She shed a few tears of joy, and there were a few from the shame of her past.

She slowly paddled back to the dock, filling her lungs with much- needed air and was breathless. She kept shaking her head trying to stay in reality. After reaching the dock and pulling her kayak up from the water, she didn't even feel that she had the energy to put it back in the shed. She took the bungee cord and tied it to the dock, thinking it would be fine until tomorrow. She headed up the hill to the house, and she felt very hungry all of a sudden. She also wanted to hear Brint's voice as quickly as possible.

Tanner reached the steps leading up to the back porch, and she stopped to grab a few pieces of wood. As she reached the top of the steps, she could hear her phone ringing. Part of her wanted to run and grab it and the other part just wanted to ignore it. She had incurred enough drama and that is what she was running from. So, she placed the wood by the fireplace on the back deck and walked inside.

Instead of going for her phone, she went to the refrigerator to pour herself a glass of iced tea. She sat down at the island, glass in one hand, staring down at the granite. The white, cream, and gray tones were mesmerizing. The ice settled in her glass and startled her. She took a sip, closed her eyes, and did her best to think of anything except that. "That," she said out loud. She pleaded with herself not to go there, but her mind was in complete power over her. Before she had time to turn her attention elsewhere, there she was Clint's arms, laying in front of the fireplace at his parent's cabin in the Wisconsin Dells, she stared into the flames as they flickered, and wood crackled. Wrapped in an old quilt, she remembered smells of cedar. He knelt beside her handing her a glass of red wine. He slid in beside her. Taking a sip and placing it on the floor beside her, she rolled toward him. She laid her head on his shoulder. Clint inhaled a deep breath taking in the fresh scent in her hair and mumbled, "I love you." Looking up at him she whispered, "I love you too."

All was perfect in her world that night. She felt safe and secure in the arms of a man she despised in childhood and had grown to love. She had even grown to love his parents and their ways. She had a complete understanding of their expectations and was willing to succumb. She had come to terms with the fact her life was going to completely mirror his mom's. She decided then and there that she was going to be the perfect wife and mother.

Tanner would do her part in supporting her husband and helping him achieve his dreams. She would join the proper clubs and host the proper parties, and her kids would have the perfect friends. They would all swim together at the country club. They would join the proper church, and she would serve on the proper committees. They would spend Sundays after church with his family, and they would visit her parents for the holidays and in the summer for their traditions she would live happily ever after. She was happier than she had ever been and soaring with emotion. She had shared herself with the man she was going to spend the rest of her life with. Clint broke her thoughts with a gentle kiss on her forehead. Brushing her cheek, he whispered in her ear, "You are my everything." His hand brushed down her neck and across her shoulder gently down her side.

CHAPTER 35

Letter Of Intent

Sitting at the desk, Brint had finally made all the notes that he could think of. He thought that the only thing left was for the most precious day of his life to get here. If he could only make time pass quicker. He decided to email Tanner.

My T,

I have waited for this day my entire life it seems. I remember when I was in high school, on a Wednesday evening specifically. I had gone to my youth night at church, and it appeared that everyone was there with their girlfriend or boyfriend that they had chosen for the month or semester. The topic this month was courtship and how to do it in the eyes of the Lord. I was there alone, of course. I didn't date much in high school. It seemed pointless, but I remember the giggles as we all filled out our worksheets.

We were answering questions like, "What are two traits that are non- negotiable in your potential mate? What are your thoughts about sex before marriage? What will you do if your partner wants sex, and you don't? What if your significant other is not a Christian? What can you do to keep yourself pure for your future husband or wife?" To me, these questions were easy. I looked around the room knowing that the majority of the couples had already crossed the line, and, more, than likely, they had not given one thought about what they wanted in their future mate. It probably didn't make a difference if their boyfriend or girlfriend was a Christian. Some were just going through the motions of looking like they cared while others were completely using this time as a way to get a date night in the middle of the school week.

I write all of this to say that I have thought about you for a really long time. I have thought about this day for a really long time. I knew in my heart what my non-negotiables were, and I also acknowledge how they have changed as time has passed. When I was in college, I was saving myself completely for marriage. I wanted a girl that was lily-white. She would be a Christian and she would be beautiful. She would be smart and have a heart of gold. It was really hard to find a girl that fit this image. They were out there, but they were mostly taken.

That is when I decided to re-negotiate my standards at the sacrifice of my faith. Needless to say, I paid the price. I found a girl. I found a lot of girls. I also found the heartache of losing many girls, as I tried to mold them into my image. I was living a double standard and realized that until I waited on God and did my best to live his will, He would never bring her to me. That is when I dove into work and church. When I couldn't be at work, I would find many ways to give my full attention to my Lord and Savior. I prayed myself to sleep so many nights. It was amazing how my prayers would answer themselves like God answering me when I would focus and listen. I realized that I needed to stop trying to find the person that I thought was perfect among all of my own imperfections.

God gave me what was perfect for me. You know that I have given away my purity as I know that you have given away yours. We have accepted that, and we have found an understanding about all the scars that we both carry with us from our past. We love one another anyway. Just as

God loves us. I believe with all of my heart that if I had not gone through

the many heartaches, then I would not have been prepared for a "perfect for me person" such as you.

T, you are perfect for me in every way. God has answered each one of my prayers in His time. I know that he has blessed me beyond measure. I certainly don't deserve an amazing woman like you, but I am so glad that God does. I cannot wait to pledge my love to you on our wedding day and for the rest of my life.

I can't wait to see you. Hurry home safely back to me.

With all the love that I have to give you today, tomorrow, and forever yours,

B-

CHAPTER 36

Camping All Alone

Responding to the GPS, he followed the instructions to exit on 108A to merge onto WIS-78 South toward Merrimac. Clint turned down the radio. The wind was enough noise as he tried his best to change the focus of his thoughts. The only voice breaking his thoughts was the GPS lady he called Helen. Helen led him right to Devil's Lake State Park. He pulled into the visitor center. The parking lot looked out over the lake, and it was a site to behold. With both hands still on the steering wheel, he laid his head down, taking in a deep breath. He needed time away, time alone. His objective was to put his thoughts in order, so he could put the past behind him.

Turning off the ignition, he drew in a deep breath and closed his eyes. Please help me get my thoughts in order. Lord what happened to me. After college, it's like I became a different person. I thought I liked that person. A drive to win in all things. This side of me, it's peaceful and I don't want it to fade. But how do I go back to my profession with the new me. I don't want to hurt anyone anymore. I don't want to be that ruthless person anymore.

This time the sound of kids laughing and running broke the silence. He climbed out of the jeep and went inside the visitor center. He loved the smell of preserved logs. He loved the slate floors which were all natural. The counter was made out of a very old tree. It had been lacquered to a shine, but you could still see the many rings. He slowed himself enough to think about the rings on the tree and wondered briefly about the years that it had seen. He thought about his years and all it had seen, and it didn't feel pure at all.

Shaking his head, he reached for a brochure about places to camp. A young woman in a park ranger uniform came up beside him and asked if she could help. He turned to her and said, "Yes, I need a place to camp for a couple of nights. I am also interested in the bike trails and maybe some kayaking?" "We can certainly accommodate you," the park ranger answered Clint. Pulling out another brochure, she opened it up, pulled out a pen from her shirt pocket and began to draw circles. She circled The Northern Lights Campground is very popular. The trees are still in full color for the fall and should not disappoint. This is the oldest campground at Devil's Lake State Park, it opened back in 1939. Three of the four bathrooms were built by the Civilian Conservation Corps. (Google- www.devilslakewisconsin.com)

"How are the bike trails this time of year?" Clint asked while he scanned the area. "Decent, considering the summer traffic at its peak," the ranger replied. "Great, I think that is all I need. I appreciate your help," **he said**. "No problem, enjoy your stay, sir," she said as she turned and walked away. Clint thought to himself, "Man, back in the day if a girl with her looks had come up next to me, I would have been all over that," he said smiling to himself as he walked back to his Jeep. Clint headed down the road a few miles to the campground. He took his time getting there. Wanting to keep his pace slow and his thoughts slower with no one to answer to and no particular time to be anywhere, he felt free.

Pulling into his camp spot, he immediately began looking for the perfect place to set up his tent. He turned off the ignition, jumped out and walked the site, kicking around leaves and a few sticks. He found the best spot, cleared away bits and pieces of debris, and marked his place for the next couple of days. He whispered to himself, "Home."

He began unloading his tent, cooler, pitched his tent first, unrolled his sleeping bag, and set up a couple of lanterns. He gathered some twigs and dried leaves to start his fire. He walked the campground gathering dead wood to keep his fire going. He knew Fall nights in Wisconsin could get pretty cold.

After the fire matured to a perfect orange with a few blue flames, he took out his tripod and hung a small iron skillet from the chain. Clint dug around in the box he had quickly packed up for something to heat up. A can of chili was the selection for the night. He had picked up a small package of hotdogs at one of the stores when he stopped for gas the last time.

He sat beside the fire carving the end of a stick carefully into a sharp point, and gently pushed the carved end through the middle of a hotdog. He then propped it against the grade to cook. He had worked hard to set up camp before dark and was ready to relax. Opening a can of Miller Light, he took an ice-cold gulp. Savoring the refreshing taste on his tongue, he inhaled slowly and filled his lungs completely with the fresh autumn air and exhaled. "I REALLY like this," he said wondering to himself why he did not do this more often. Listening to the crackle of the fire, he stretched back on his Kelty camp chair, folded his fingers behind his head and closed his eyes.

It didn't take long until an aching feeling formed in his chest. His eyes popped open, and he sat up quickly to void the image and the thought from his head. He kept blinking, doing his best to clear his mind. Grabbing his stick, he used to stoke the fire, he adjusted his hotdog and stirred his chili. He stood up and walked to the outer edge of his campsite. The sun had just dipped below the horizon on the lake, and he could see the peach-colored sparkles it was reflecting on the water. It now looked black, and the moon had begun to claim it's time to cast a magnificent picture of diamonds that looked as if they were dancing off the waves as they finally made it to the shore.

He could hear the boats in the distance making their way back to the docks after a fun day on the lake. Clint tried to specifically focus on each scene before him to block the thoughts that were doing their best to push their way through. He just didn't want to go there right now, and he absolutely could not allow himself to go there. While the drive was relatively effortless, his thoughts had completely drained him, mentally and physically.

CHAPTER 37

Soul Search

Tanner stretched out across the granite. She pressed her cheek against the cold surface, closing her eyes for a moment. Pleading in a soft whispered tone, Please Lord. She felt like her emotions were playing tug- of-war inside of her. The worst part about it was that these feelings were so intertwined, that it would be like trying to untangle the world's biggest ball of yarn.

She prayed to herself and forced herself off the countertop. She heard her phone buzzing, and she didn't want to think about answering it. Finally, it stopped, and she felt relieved. Then it started again. As she walked toward it, she thought, no you came here to get away and relax before the wedding. The objective was to unplug and since I have been here all that has happened is every time my phone rings I have faced with some sort of situation. Which has led to another situation, one that she felt she was going to need to put to sleep. Forever.

CHAPTER 38

Just Hangin' out With Andy

Brint called Andy. He thought some guy time might help keep his mind off how badly he was missing Tanner. "Hey buddy, do you want to meet up for a beer?" Brint asked. "Sure! What time?" Andy responded. "Six work for you?" he suggested. "It will. Is everything all right?" Andy agreed but was concerned. "Yeah man, it's just a little, too quiet for my liking," Brint reassured him. "Same place?" Andy confirmed. "You got it," he said back with confidence.

Andy had been the person Brint had shared with although he wasn't the sharing type. That's one of the things he held most precious about his relationship with Tanner. He felt comfortable with her and had told her details about his life that he had never told anyone. While getting ready, his mind began to wander to the first time he had met Tanner's parents. The whole family had gathered at the lake house to watch the Tennessee/Florida game. (Her mother's Alma mater was University of Tennessee.) It was also Lexi's birthday weekend.

As soon as they entered the front door, they all stood up and greeted them with hugs and warm smiles. "We've heard so much about you!" her sister shrieked. Brint loved the excitement, but most of all it was overwhelmingly obvious how close and connected they were as a family. He remembered feeling a part of them immediately. It wasn't completely surprising, because Tanner talked about them all the time-telling stories and memories. So, he felt like he knew a little or a lot about each of them.

There was a quaint fire burning in the living room. The television was blaring ESPN College Game Day, which happened to be filmed from the University of Tennessee that Saturday. He could smell something being smoked...he figured pork. He could also smell a maple scent in the air. There were a couple of pies on the island. Of course, there were pitchers of tea, which didn't surprise him either. He was in the South.

He could see the lake through the wall of sliding, glass doors. He thought her mom must like candles. They seemed to be lit everywhere, even in the bathroom as he recalled. There were quilts on the back of each couch, which were all very warn from use. He imagined they had been in the family for decades. They were probably made by Great Grandmothers. There were family photos tucked here and there of the family at UT games, boat outings, ski trips, beach trips, and much more. Some of them included her grandparents, but never without the family of four. They ranged from ages of four or five years through college he assumed. He loved seeing the pictures of Tanner as she grew up. He made it a point to look at each throughout the evening. His family didn't have many family pictures.

At about half time, the meat came off the smoker, and it was obviously a grand event. Spencer was decked out in his apron that read, 'smokin hot,' and everyone cheered when he came through the door. Oddly, we ate off of the good china. Tanner mentioned that it was her grandmother's. Some ate in the living room, some of us ate at the kitchen table, but Tanner and I ate outside. There was a slight breeze coming off of the lake, and there was a fire in the fire pit. It was still very warm outside.

He could not remember a time that he felt like he was surrounded by love and genuine down to earth people...it was pure, simple, and grand all at once. His heart felt full. He had been falling in love with Tanner over the last year and this moment in time seemed to validate his feelings. He turned to look at Tanner as she was taking a bit of her corn, butter dripping down her chin, and juice squirting her on the face. Her hair was whisking her face in the breeze. He knew without a doubt that he would and could love her forever.

Andy chose a table near the window but also angled to see the television. He loved college football, no matter who was playing. He knew Brint would be arriving any minute and went ahead and ordered him a Miller Lite. He ordered a half order of fully loaded cheese fries and twenty hot wings. He figured that would be enough to get them started. He waived Brint down as soon as he hit the door. Andy considered Brint to be his best friend. He was loyal, and he had stuck with him through all his divorces. He never judged and seemed to keep him from self-destruction. Brint appreciated their friendship.

As soon as Brint arrived, he quickly spotted Andy. The food and beverages arrived almost at the same time. "Thanks, great timing," Brint said with a bit of excitement in his voice. He was starved. Taking a sip of his beer he began talking almost frantically. He was so happy to have some company. He didn't even realize that he had not given Andy a chance to respond. He was suddenly very thankful Andy was a good listener. "I don't mean to cut you off, you want another beer?" asked Andy. "Why not?" Brint countered his question.

Continuing his story without leaving out a detail, Brint was sharing his memory from earlier with Andy. He wanted his friend to see what he saw and feel what he felt. "Later that evening, T and I went out on the pontoon. The sun was beginning to set. It was the perfect evening. We rode around the lake. Tanner was pointing out the cliff she and her sister used to climb and jump from. She told stories of how she learned to water ski, then wake boarded, and had countless water tubing memories. Her eyes danced as she

shared. I could have listened all night. I remember wondering what our family life would look like. I hadn't even asked for her hand yet, but I knew I would. Now we are getting married next weekend. My prayers are being answered," Brint finished with the biggest smile on his face.

CHAPTER 39
Feelings

Clint polished off his hotdog, chili, and beer. He was contemplating opening one more and then decided he better not. He sat motionless, staring into the bright orange and blue embers. The flames had disappeared, although there was still immense heat radiating from the fire. He was mesmerized by way the embers would take turns illuminating as the air would hit them.

The darkness had finally arrived. Clint added some wood and stoked the fire once more before heading to bed. Snuggling into his bag for the night, he reached over and turned off the lantern. It was pitch black. He could hear the night. All the insects seemed to be in harmony, and it was an amazing lullaby. Clint closed his eyes, took in a deep breath, and tried to focus on relaxing his neck, shoulders, torso, legs, and feet. It was a method he had read about, but for some reason, it never seemed to completely relax him. He tried to pray and felt a little better, but he just couldn't quite get there this evening.

It was the first night since he had such deep conversations with the Lord that he was having difficulty truly letting go and letting down. He then tried to focus on the darkness. Closing his eyes, all he could see was black.

Slowly he drifted off. It wasn't long before the darkness that always found him began to take over. Creeping over him like a thick fog. It rolled around his throat and then finally enveloped his entire body.

As the visions became clearer, he could see a tree by itself in a field. It was damp and cold. The leaves were falling from the tree one by one. He could see something moving in the tree, but he couldn't make out what it was. At the base of the tree, he could see a girl. He didn't recognize her. She was a beautiful girl, sitting there with her knees pulled to her chest. She looked sad and distant. As he tried to walk closer to the tree he felt as if he were walking up a steep hill. He felt breathless as his legs grew heavier with each step. He yelled out for her, and she was gone in an instant. Clint kept walking and it got harder and harder for him to place one foot in front of the other the closer he got to the tree.

The fog became thicker and denser with each breath. The leaves continued to fall one by one until the tree was completely bare. Upon finally reaching what appeared to be once a thriving oak, it was beginning to lose its bark and began to crumble. He woke suddenly feeling suffocated and very tired. He quickly turned on the lantern and reached for his phone. It was only midnight. Blinking, he looked again. It felt like he had been asleep for hours.

Feeling a bit panicked by the nightmarish dream and then waking to find that it was only midnight when he had fought so hard to go to sleep, he cursed into the night.

This was not the first time he had experienced this feeling. In fact, it had been the norm for the past couple of years. On occasion, he would have a dream about Tanner, and it had been welcomed. He often woke up from those dreams ready to conquer the world in a day. It was that feeling he had a longing for. He began to pray, but it was like his thoughts kept getting interrupted by a flickering glimpse, or sudden feeling, of dread. It was like moments of his life were flashing before his eyes, and with each came a jolt. It was almost like each memory was giving him an electric shock. He tried to focus harder on finding the peace he had suddenly found, and it was like it had disappeared from existence.

He thought to himself, I am worthy of peace. I am worthy. He turned off the lantern and laid back down. He pulled his sleeping bag around himself as tightly as he could, closed his eyes, and fell back asleep. This time there was nothing. No thoughts, no feelings, just nothing, and he recognized how alone he was.

CHAPTER 40

Wine Time

Tanner looked at her phone, she just couldn't help it. It was Lex. Thinking to herself, "I absolutely do not have the energy to go through the details one more time." She decided against building the fire she had looked forward to. She slid the glass doors shut and locked them. Grabbing a quilted pillow from the chair, she headed toward the couch. Pulling the blanket from the back of the couch, she laid down. She turned the television on and flipped through a few channels. HGTV, back to OWN. Thinking to herself, "Now there is an interesting woman. I love Oprah!" Then back to HGTV. Chip and Joanna Gaines, again to herself she thought, "What an amazing couple!"

Settling on an NFL game, which was a rerun, but she didn't care. She decided to just leave it. There was something about the cabin and the sound of football in the background that made her feel comfortable. She pulled the afghan around her. It had been made with a heavy, cotton-like yarn, and it smelled like home. She made herself cozy, and, before she could think one more thought, she had fallen into a peaceful, comfortable, deep sleep.

Tanner was awakened by the television. She opened her eyes, trying to focus, she heard the words, "We bring you a special report this evening."

She closed her eyes again, doing her best to get back to the place she was just moments before when she heard, "Investigators may have uncovered a motive behind the apparent suicide of Leonard Copeland. We will have more on this breaking story at 11." She sat up quickly. Moments later her phone began to ping and ping. She picked it up. It was Lex, Dad, and Sara.

"What on earth?" Tanner said out loud. She opened the first text from Lex.

> Lex: Hey T, I think I might head your way in the morning. If I leave at 9 my time, I will be there by 1 your time. C U soon.

Tanner's mind began working overtime again. "I just want to be by myself," she thought. "Damn it!" Tanner said, shaking her head no. Scrolling to the next text, which was from her dad.

> Dad: T, turn on the news at 11. Isn't Leonard Copeland involved with the case you have been working on? Story is at 11. Call me! Love you bunches, Dad.

Tanner loved the way her dad seemed to always be on top of

things and followed all of her cases. It was like being in practice with him. Partners. Sometimes she wished that she could talk her dad out of retirement. He always ended his texts with, love you bunches, just as he signed all of his cards back in the day...love you bunches. It was his signature to her. She wondered how he signed off with Lex. It really didn't matter; this was theirs, and she cherished it.

She picked up the remote and scheduled the television to begin recording the 11 o'clock news. Channel 10, her favorite. She loved the sound of the jingle. She loved hearing her favorite news anchor. Some had retired, and she missed the sound of their voices as it reminded her of her childhood. The news was never missed. During her time in Chicago, she never remembered something like the news creating a nostalgic feeling like it did when they spent time at the cabin. She wondered if this was strange that she liked hearing the Heartland Series. She always learned something about her heritage, and just the sound of that jingle, sometimes stirred those feelings as well.

Bill Landry's voice was one that could not be duplicated, and it was part of her story. She loved it when they covered the Appalachian Museum and the history that had been preserved: Strait from the Heart. She loved Tennessee. Taking a moment to reminisce. She then scrolled to the text from Sara.

> Sara: Tanner, call me when you can.
> The phones have been blowing up
> since about 4. I just wanted to fill
> you in.

She briefly wondered who she needed to call first, Lex to tell her to stay in Nashville, or Sara to stay in touch with her livelihood. She rang Lex first.

"Hey!" Tanner answered. "Lex, I'm glad I caught you! You don't need to come. I'm good," she said. Cutting her off, "Too late! I'm here!" Lexi said. Suddenly, she heard the front door opening, confirmed that she was too late. Tanner hung up and met her sister in the entry way. Lex dropped her bags, wrapped her arms around her sister and squeezed as tight as she could. She made note that T wasn't letting go. She knew her sister. This was code for, there is something up. "T are you really, OK?" her sister mumbled something. "T?" Lexi asked. Hearing her delicate sniffles about broke her heart. She loved her sister dearly and had always looked up to her and knew her sis to be strong on the inside and with a huge heart that loved fiercely. Lexi also knew her sister would pretend that everything was just fine on the outside when she was completely falling apart on the inside. This was something that she had learned how to do back in college. She just held her as she let her feeling pour out.

Feeling Tanner relaxing, she slowly began to pull away to get a glimpse of her sister's tears that were streaming down her face. Looking into her eyes, she knew there was a list of things that needed attention, and she knew without a doubt that she had made the right decision to listen to her gut feeling. Her gut feeling also told her that there was something dark brewing and it was driving her crazy not to be able to pinpoint the ominous thoughts and feeling swirling in her head and heart.

Lex left her bags and took her sister's hand. She led her to the couch, and they sat down, and wiped the tears from her sister's eyes reminding her to breathe. She picked up the blanket and wrapped it around her shoulders.

Giving her a moment, she just sat there in silence.

Tanner began after taking a deep sigh. Your text said, "You would come tomorrow? I'm so glad that you are here. I have no clue where to begin. But before I do. I need to call Sara," Tanner said. "OK, you do that and I'm going to get my things put away and grab a glass of tea," Lexi said. "No, you better grab the wine. Tea is not strong enough right now. And don't forget to pour some for me. I am going to step outside for a moment," Tanner responded. Looking at Tanner scurrying around, Lexi confirmed yet again to herself, "I am so glad I didn't wait!"

Lexi picked up her bags and headed down the hallway. Feeling the slate floor beneath her feet and seeing the rustic sconces on the walls that lighted the way to her room gave her a feeling of peace. So many memories were coming back, and it made her feel like she had almost stepped back in time. She flipped on the lights in her room. The lighting was cozy and complimented the natural light that was still coming through the window that stretched from the floor to the half cathedral ceiling. The sun was setting and was casting an orange hue on the cream-colored walls.

She placed her bags on the folding, mahogany, luggage rack. This had been her grandmother's, and she paused a moment missing her. She closed the closet doors and turned to the dresser. There she found some shorts that had been left there from the last time she visited. She found her rugged Vanderbilt t-shirt. It had been washed so many times that the letters had begun to fade. Lexi grabbed her makeup bag and headed to the bathroom. She turned on the warm water had reached for a washcloth. She loved the way her mom kept them rolled up in a shallow woven basket on the granite counter. Of course, it all coordinated as her mother would have it no other way. Sometimes it got on her nerves and other times the consistency made her feel safe.

When she wet the washcloth, it smelled of Tide and Downy. This was almost a trademark smell that reminded her of home. Her grandmother washed laundry with the same two products, and she loved how it made her feel when the fragrance filled her as she washed her face. Finally, feeling refreshed from her drive, she turned off the lights. The eerie sound of her dad's voice in her mind became ever present. "Turn off the light Lexi!" he would yell several times daily as the girls were growing up. As she turned the corner to the living room, she could see her sister frantically trying to get back through the sliding glass door. She thought to herself, 'Oh, boy!' She rarely saw Tanner in a frantic state, and, at this point, it was almost at the full come apart stage.

"Oh, my gosh, Lexi, sit down, oh, my goodness sit down! Did you get the wine?" Tanner asked. "T, calm down. You are going to hyperventilate. I am going to get the wine and you start talking. OK?" Lexi said. "Red, no white, is there any more Riesling?" Tanner asked. "Yes!" she yelled. "I want that!" Tanner yelled back. Lexi started toward the kitchen with the wine order. She passed the built-in, wine rack and grabbed a bottle of Chateau St. Michelle. Their mom always kept a couple of bottles of the favorites among the more sophisticated brands. Cheap wine, yes, but tasty and that's all that matters, she thought. As she began to pour their glasses, Tanner started. At first all Lexi could think was how on earth this would have looked if she had not come. She also thought what on earth does she do when I am not around. Shaking her head, she picked up the two glasses and walked back to the couch. Tanner all but grabbed the glass out of her hand. "Sit, sit!" she commanded.

CHAPTER 41

Confiding In Andy

"Man, come on, you sure you haven't been watching Hallmark since she's been gone?" Andy chuckled as he took a sip of his beer. "Hey just because you didn't find love on the first try doesn't mean everyone else's relationship is a joke," Brint sarcastically came back. "I don't mean for you to take it that way. It's just that it sounds so perfect," Andy said. "It was perfect," Brint looked down into his beer bottle realizing that he had already finished the last sip. "What do you mean it was perfect?" Andy asked. "It was, it is!" Brint exclaimed. "OK!" Andy said with a laugh.

Brint started "There is this guy, Clint, Clint Winstead. Have you ever heard of him?" he asked Andy. "Heard of him, man he is one of the most well-known attorneys in the state. He is known for being a shyster, so was his dad. They don't lose, and they are known for doing whatever it takes to win," Andy said with a serious tone.

"I know!" Brint threw back some peanuts. Shaking his head slightly and smirking. "What's the deal?" Andy asked. "He is who is representing the clients in this big case Tanner has been working on. She has been completely consumed. I don't think she has realized that I have noticed. She has been practically hyperventilating in her sleep. She has been taking the long way home, stopping at the loop because

she has needed 'me' time, she says, and…"

Andy cut Brint off because he was beginning to ramble, and it isn't a good look on him. "And, she has been stressed and just needing to burn off some pent-up energy after work," Andy continued. "And the hyperventilating," Brint cut him off "Maybe she is stressed over her ex?" "What!" Andy exclaimed. "Her ex, Clint Winstead?" "Whoa! What? Tanner and Clint?" Andy said skeptically. "No way, that guy has a reputation, and it's not a good one," he continued. "That's what I am finding out! How do you know so much about him?" Brint asked. "I read the papers, and when I was working at the police department, I took a report on him. He evidently hadn't come to terms with the fact that his then ex-girlfriend had moved on. He waited on the guy to drop her off, and he jumped him outside of her apartment. He was full of himself. He was yelling about who he was, who his dad was and saying he would have my badge. You know, the usual, I am big and bad and above the law stuff. So, Tanner really dated him?" Andy was trying to understand.

"Evidently, it was pretty serious while they were in college, and then it turned ugly. He treated her pretty bad in the end. He really made it difficult for her to trust again," Brint explained. "Did she share all of this with you?" Andy asked. "No, that's just it, she always talked about this guy. She told me stories, and every time it would make my blood boil. I could not understand how someone could do her that way. She says that it made her stronger and a better person, and she somehow gives him some piece of credit for her success in her career. All of this time when she would share, I was able to listen and somehow, while I knew this guy was real, he didn't have a name. So, I was able to just listen. I talked to Lexi, her sister, the other night because she had me really worried. I just could not handle it any longer. She shared all the gory details with me and gave him a name. Clint Winstead. Now, I understand her obsession with the case and her need to win this case and in a way beat him in court. I could never tell her Lexi told me. Lexi promised me that she would never tell although she and her sister don't keep secrets. I think this is safe, because she is on my side. She sees how perfect T and I are for each other. She knows that I am good for her and, believe me, I know without a shadow of a doubt that Tanner is good for me. I have tried to let the information become a part of allowing me to understand her and use it to be able to make her life just that much better. So far it has worked," Brint said.

"Well, that is what you should do. Respect her feelings, and, when she is ready to share, she will," Andy said. "She shared with me last night that he called her. She said that it was a friendly conversation and that he was just sharing that the case was basically dead. No pun intended," he said. "Then you have to trust that's all it was and move past this. You are getting married. Married to one fine lady, and you will have the rest of your lives to learn about one another. Take it from me. Put the past in the past. There is a reason it is in the past, and there is one thing for certain, there is no future in the past. Believe me. Not to mention that you trust her, and she trusts you. If you go questioning her about this call, you will open the door for negative energy to seep in and there is no room for that in any relationship," Andy encouraged. "I would trust her with my life! I know she would be completely honest with me. I would never put her in the position to feel like I didn't trust her," Brint said.

CHAPTER 42

Clint's Camping Trip

When Clint woke that morning, he could tell that it was early, because the humidity had not yet set in. The dampness from the dew on the tent had not yet turned to steam. He folded up his sleeping bag and cleared out the tent. He took his tent and the items that were inside to the Jeep. Returning to his campsite, he gathered what was left of the wood and started a small fire. He made himself a cup of coffee, he scrambled some eggs and toast, and grabbed an apple out of the cooler. Clint took a huge bite. He was starving this morning, and he imagined that it was from the restless night that he had.

Clint tried to remember the specifics of his dream. In his heart he knew the girl in his dream was Tanner. Although he didn't want to admit it, because it was a reflection of his ugliness toward her. A lump began to form in his throat before he took a sip of coffee, and he pushed it away with a swallow. His heart felt tight, and he fought that with a stretch. He wasn't particularly fond of feeling weak or out of control, and these feelings made him feel just that.

He practically ate his breakfast whole, as he took one last look at his campsite to ensure it reflected a place that no one had been. Clean-up was important to him, and he wished others took it just as seriously. He took a moment to think about how God had created the ground he slept on and the sun that was coming up over the ridge, the warmth he was feeling, and the cool, September, morning breeze that was fighting for part in the morning dance. It was a brief but special moment for him. It reminded him that he wasn't alone. All of these things were there to let him know that God was never far away. In fact, he was surrounded by Him. He was thankful for the moment that he took time to realize this. He felt the grip on his heart begin to loosen, and he began to feel happy and alive.

After climbing into his Jeep, he pulled out the guide that he had picked up at check in and began to lay out the plan for his day. He glanced at his phone fighting the urge to pick it up. For the last five years he began each morning with looking at a text or email as soon as his eyes opened each morning. He took care of the most important items first and returned any urgent calls, usually to his secretary as she was at the office at 6:00 a.m. each morning and stayed on call 24-7. He appreciated her support, and without her, he would be a mess. Clients absolutely loved her. He was lucky to have her, and he knew it, although he knew now that he had never shown her.

He made a mental note to discuss a raise and some additional vacation time with her as soon as he returned. This, he knew, was the right thing to do and would do regularly from this point forward. He felt a pang of guilt knowing that she took such loving care of him and was so passionate about their firm, and he had never given her a single raise for her efforts. There had been no reward for a job well done. He briefly wondered what she must actually think of him. He also realized that this was a pattern of thought that he had not been used to. In the past he thought about himself and his gain in every situation. He made yet another mental note that he was letting that being go forever. His mind was calling him all sorts of ugly names, and he quickly put a stop to it. He recognized his self-talk must stay positive, and he no longer would associate with those descriptions.

After picking up the phone and quickly locking it in his console, avoiding even a glance, he felt pleased. He started up the narrow winding road to a trail he had found on the guide. It looked like it would provide some challenge, but still easy enough to find his relaxation. It also appeared to have some great views along the way. He imagined that he would spend about four hours on the trail. He parked his Jeep in the shade and unhooked his bike. He filled water into his Camelback and tucked some energy snacks in the pockets. Clint strapped on his helmet and other biking gear to set out for an amazing day in God's country.

Clint felt the burn in his legs as he navigated his way up the winding path. His head was filled with determination, and his body was drenched with sweat! Just ahead, he could see a clearing in the trees. It appeared to be a common spot as the undergrowth had been trampled on so much that it had turned into a mud hole. A very narrow trail had been created that led to an overlook. His body was telling him, in no uncertain terms, that he was due for a break. He could feel his pulse pounding and it was almost echoing in his head. Sweat was dripping profusely down his brow, neck, and chest. He pulled the cooling towel from his Camelback pack and wiped his face and neck. There was a slight breeze, and, when the air hit his body, it enveloped him concentrating on the dampest parts. Before, this would have been an enjoyable non-event. However, this time he acknowledged that God had provided for his need to cool down, and he ultimately felt thankful.

Walking toward the clearing, he realized that the trail turned to a solid piece of rock beneath his feet. The trail grew wider and wider with each stride. Suddenly he was taken aback by the image before him. You could see as far away as the eye could perform! It was as if he were looking at an expensive piece of art. His eyes were darting here and there taking in every color, shadow, and depth. The sky was a crisp, vibrant, light blue.

He let out a chuckle thinking to himself, Crayon, Sky Blue. There were still several shades of green present, although the bright oranges, reds, and yellows were making their debut. No doubt Fall was making its grand arrival. The longer he looked the more he felt his breath being taken away in awe. He couldn't remember a view so beautiful in all his life. Except Tanner.

Pushing that thought away as quickly as it had come, he continued to stare. This is what people mean when they say, God is an amazing artist. He remembered thinking this was such a silly statement. He realized that he was the one being silly. God is an artist, and he gives us these views to remind us of his love and power.

It was difficult to turn away from such a beautiful sight. He thought to himself, how do I keep this image alive in my mind and in my heart? He looked up toward the sky and smiled. This was a gesture that seemed to be repeating itself these last few days! It was a gesture of thankfulness, and he promised himself he would never forget.

CHAPTER 43

Tanner's Confession

As Lexi sat, she grabbed one of the many blankets lying around and pulled it across her legs. "Tann, first you need to slow down. I need to be able to keep up. I don't think I have ever seen you this worked up. Well, maybe once, but we'll not go there. I want you to take it from the beginning," she asked. "OK, well, you know the Copeland land development I have been working on. I represent the buyers," Tanner began the story. Lex was shaking her head up and down. "Have you seen any of the news?" She asked Lexi. "Yes, but I don't know details and I still don't know what you had so undone, "she looked confused.

"Well, the defendant was found dead," Tanner added. "Yes, I know that much," she answered. "And I believe I have told you Clint, as in Winstead, is the lead attorney!" Tanner continued. This is why I have not been me in months. Is this all coming together so far? And the timing is a whole different subject!" Tanner rambled.

Oh Lex, the hits just keep coming! I just got off the phone with Sara, and she told me that the state police just left the office and were there to inform me that there was going to be further investigation into the death of Mr. Copeland and wanted to ask me some questions. She then told me that the buyers had contacted her and that there has been a body found on the property! They would like to find a way to back out of the whole deal and drop the lawsuit," Tanner continued.

"Keep going, this is getting good, "Lexi said with curiosity as she leaned in toward Tanner. "That's just it, I don't know anything else. So, all I know is I have worked my ass off for months because there was no way on this green earth that I was going to let Clint beat me on this. Not to mention that a defeat against him and the Copeland family would be a huge boost for my career and our firm. You have no clue what my emotions have gone through to gear up to face him in a court room. All the emotions and memories that have been drudged from the depths of my soul that I have had to face head on, while trying to plan a wedding and keep Brint from recognizing that the case was getting my full attention. I feel like I have almost been running a split personality scheme, and that's not all. Clint called me last night! He called my number. He had the guts to dial my digits," Tanner said with such relief since she had finally said it out loud.

"Stop it! T, you forget the case! You know I don't understand all of that stuff anyway," Lexi reminded her. Both girls paused just long enough to take a sip of their wine and then Lex started. "Clint Winstead called you. What did he say?" Lexi asked with a motherly tone. "This is the really weird part which shouldn't be, but it is. He was sweet. There was a genuine tone in his voice," Tanner said as she cut her eyes away from Lexi's. "Shut up, Clint doesn't have a genuine word in his vocabulary," she laughed out loud. "Seriously, he was apologizing and telling me about how I was the first person that he called to share about his new relationship with the Lord. Evidently, he and Copeland were good friends, and he was close with the family. He was taking this loss hard it seemed. It changed him, he said, somehow. If you could have just heard him Lexi," Tanner said.

"Tanner, you are getting married in a matter of days. Don't you dare think about seeing him!" she said with a sharp tone. "He knows I am getting married, and it wasn't like that at all. He told me he was sorry for how he treated me. He also said he was going to call his parents and apologize to them. It was all very real and from his actual heart. I always knew it was there," Tanner said still trying to not look directly at Lexi.

"Well, good for him. Let him go ahead and beg and plead with his apologies. You have found a wonderful man, and he cares for you deeply," Lexi reminded her. "I know he does, he's my best friend," Tanner said.

"What? You know what I mean," she said. "Yeah, yeah, yeah, you leave Clint alone. I do not trust him. I certainly do not trust him with you or your heart. I have to say that I am kind of disappointed that you are not going to get the chance to make a fool of him in court," Lexi said as she laughed. "I was kind of looking forward to my day too," Tanner agreed. "But back to Copeland, how crazy is this that a case I am involved with has suicide, potential murder, and an unknown dead body?"

CHAPTER 44

Girl Talk

The two girls talked into the early morning hours until they had drifted off to sleep, piled up on the couch just like they used to do when they were young girls, challenging each other with who was staying up all night. Except this time when they awakened with the morning sunlight beaming through the living room, there was no aroma of coffee, syrup, cinnamon, or bacon. They yawned and stretched as they stirred to life. Tanner stood first and headed directly to the kitchen. "Lex, coffee?" she said holding up the empty coffee pot.

"Sure, do we have anything to eat?" Lexi asked. "Are you nuts, mom stocked the house top to bottom like I was going to be here a month. There are some eggs, bacon, and potatoes. Why don't we make some fried potatoes?" she asked. "I haven't had fried potatoes in ages, which sounds so good," Lexi agreed. "Me either, I do my best to eat healthy at home. But, when in the South," and they said together, "Eat like in the South!"

Lexi placed the bowl of scrambled eggs on the kitchen table. Tanner brought over the bacon and a plate of buttered toast. Lexi retreated to the refrigerator for jelly and fruit. They both poured a small glass of orange juice and then sat staring at the spread of food before them. "Are we going eat all of this?" Tanner asked. "We sure are!" she replied as she stuffed a bite of egg in her mouth.

"So where did we leave off?" Tanner was trying to remember. "I think you were saying something about how crazy the people in your case were," Lexi said with a mouth full. "NO! They are not crazy, the case, well, the story around the case had become insanely crazy," she explained. "I still can't get past Clint calling you. I guess I was so shocked about that part that I was drifting in and out of exactly what you were saying about the case," Lexi said.

"Seriously, Clint is not at the top of my priority list these days," Tanner said with relief she could be over him.

"So, what is exactly going on with this case?" Lexi asked. "Well, it was really a straightforward, business deal, until Clint's clients decided they wanted to back out of the contract under a technicality that wasn't covered in the contract. The case was easy. I could do that part in my sleep. I let myself get stressed, because I know that Clint has a reputation of not playing by the rules, and I seriously would not put it past him to pay someone to plant a dead body on the land just to stall the case or to give my clients a reason to just drop it," Tanner said with a sigh. "Do you really think he would do something so horrific?" Lexi asked in shock. "No, not really, but he does not play well with others. He can be dirty when it comes to winning," she said as she looked away pondering the past memories of his dirty deeds.

"Well, I know you play by the rules, and, for that, you have always been recognized. Also, I know that you would have won that case fair and square which would have made your victory that much more of an accomplishment. Cheaters never really win, and winners never cheat," Lexi said. "True! Listen, I swore that I was going to completely unplug when I arrived, but that was before all of this broke loose. I really need to call Sara and find out what is really going on. I need to put a plan in place before I truly get my day started. Then, when I am done. I want to spend the day with you. Are we cool?" Tanner asked.

"That sounds perfect," Lexi said as she stared at Tanner in admiration. She had always admired her sister. She was a great role model, and she was so proud of being Tanner's little sister. Lexi knew she had made the right decision to come to the lake. After finishing and putting away the dishes, Tanner and Lexi retreated to their bedrooms to freshen up for the day. They had decided on taking the kayaks out to the point.

Tanner took a moment to check her phone, there were three messages.

One from her mom which read:

> Mom: I hope you girls are having fun
> and don't stay up all night. Love Mom.
> Tanner smiled at the fact that her mom
> always had their best interests at heart.
> No matter what it was.

The next message was from Brint,

Brint: T, I love you, I miss you and I
can't wait to see you. Love you with all
my heart B.

Tanner felt her heart do a little flip. She took a moment to recognize just how blessed she was to have a man tell her he loved her in so many ways. She whispered to herself, "Thank you, God!" She knew without a shadow of a doubt that He was completely responsible for the many blessings in her life and for this one in particular. His timing was perfect, and He sent her exactly what she needed. She knew their chance meeting was not an accident but a perfectly direct play by no other, her Lord and Savior. With a full heart, she tapped on the next message from Sara. It read: Tanner, I know you don't get the local news there, but you need to call me as soon as you get this message. I just think you need to know. Without hesitation, she turned to sit on the bed that was still made from the day before suddenly feeling like maybe she just needed to crawl in it. Resisting the feeling to hide, she dialed Sara immediately.

"Hey, Sara! Do I even want to ask?" Tanner said hesitating. "Ha, Ha, funny girl, this case is getting pretty interesting. You may want to look it up for yourself, but the investigation around Leonard Copeland's suicide is heating up. Evidently, he was under investigation for falsifying legal documents, forgery, blackmail and now murder!" Sara explained. "I want to say I am shocked, but on the other hand I am not. Have you talked to Mr. Holbrook?" Tanner asked. "Yes, yesterday evening, and obviously, he doesn't want this property any longer. He said as soon as he finds another one, he will let you know," she continued. "Fine, no problem. Have you talked to Mr. Winstead?" she asked...just that name still made her stomach tighten. "Yes, but not about the case really," Tanner said. "Oh?" Sara sounded surprised. "Yes, long, really long story. We will do lunch as soon as I get back. So, speaking of getting back home. Lex came in last night, and I think I need to just stay here until the wedding is over. I don't have much on my schedule, a couple lunch meetings and one dinner meeting. Would you care to clear those? We will reschedule as soon as I return from my honeymoon." That sounded so bizarre, "Honeymoon?" she said to herself, but it was a little louder than she had planned.

"What?" Sara asked confused. "Oh, nothing really, it just sounds so strange to say honeymoon. I mean I am getting married. I just never thought I would find someone that could make me feel the way Brint does. But I did," Tanner said. "I know you are going to be very happy. I am so excited for you both. I will clear your schedule, and I guess I will see you in about three weeks?" Sara said. "I guess so. Hey, after you get things tidy at the office, forward the office phone to the answering service and take some time for you," Tanner said. "Seriously?" Sara asked excitedly. "Absolutely, you have worked so hard. I know that I don't tell you like I should, but I appreciate you and the job that you do on a daily basis. You always go above and beyond for me and our clients because we are a team. Don't forget that. I cannot do what I do without you. Now, get to work clearing that calendar and go do something fun. We will exchange stories as soon as I return. Deal!" Tanner said. "Deal! Tanner!" Sara agreed. "Yes," she answered. "Thank you!" Sara said with a grateful heart. "Get busy!" she said with a laugh.

Tanner hung up the phone and smiled. She again knew how blessed she was to have Sara as her right hand. She sat there a while longer fighting the urge to pull up the Chicago Tribune, and wanted to so badly, but she also wanted to just put all of this chaos behind her and move forward. With that thought she decided not to linger too long and walked toward the shower. After opening up the window to let the breeze in, she adjusted the temperature of her water and leaned her hair back under the warmth. Not too warm, it actually had a hint of cold to it. It felt refreshing and reminded her how much she enjoyed the outdoor shower downstairs and how amazing it felt after a hot day on the lake.

Suddenly, she was jolted by an image in that very shower and quickly opened her eyes to steady herself. Her heart felt like it had been hit with a slight jolt of electricity like she had been shocked. She immediately turned the water as cold as she could to completely bring herself to the present. A piece of her felt anger and a piece felt a pain from the past. As dull as it was, she was not happy that it had a space at all. She quickly turned off the shower and grabbed the towel. Trying to focus on the amazing day she was about to share with her sister, she hurried through her routine. She put her hair in a ponytail and wiped some sunscreen on her cheeks and forehead. She flipped off the lights and got dressed at mock speed.

While she was placing her foot in her chaos, she yelled. "Lex! Are you about ready?" Her voice echoed through the hallway as if she were on a speaker. She heard her sister faintly from the other room. "Almost!" The cabin sounded alive this morning and it was a comforting feeling. Her heart began to slow, and she felt her blood pressure begin to decline. As she stood, she caught a glimpse of herself in the mirror. Thinking to herself that she looked rattled, but it was because she was rattled. "Tan, you have got to get your stuff together girl," Tanner mumbled to herself. Just then, Lexi popped her head around the corner. "I'm good, are you?" Lexi said. "Yes, let's get out of here!" Tanner said with a bit of relief.

CHAPTER 45

Stay Positive

Waking with the sunlight, Brint popped out of bed. He felt better this morning. He had enjoyed his time the night before and had no doubts this morning. He hopped in the shower and began whistling. He laughed out loud because he never whistled, much less in the shower. He hopped out almost as quickly as he hopped in. He was eager to get his day started. After feeding the cat that was circling his legs, obviously missing Tanner, he fixed his coffee and sat down at the kitchen island. He was keenly aware something was missing. It was Tanner. He was also aware that he was happy when he thought about her and that he missed her terribly. He took a moment to recognize how thankful he was to have found her, and that she was going to be his wife.

While not an outwardly religious person, he believed in his Lord and Savior without a shadow of a doubt. He knew he was saved, which had happened when he was fourteen. He will never forget it, and he knew that God had prepared him for Tanner. He called his brother then his dad just to check in. Everyone had been fitted for their tux and was ready for the upcoming nuptials. They didn't have an elaborate conversation. They never did. But that was how they were. Andy had been fitted and he was ready.

He looked at the checklist once more on his phone just to make sure he had done everything that was required of him. Travel Agency, check. Rehearsal Dinner, check. It all seemed to be playing out perfectly. This made him a bit uneasy as there had to be a hiccup somewhere. No, he thought to himself. There is no room for negativity. Quickly pushing that out of his mind, he took the last sip of coffee and rose to place it in the sink. He quickly turned on the faucet to fill the cup and turned it off. With that he grabbed his keys out of the basket and headed out the door. Arriving at the sidewalk he decided that he wasn't going to drive anywhere. He placed his keys in his pocket and walked toward the park.

CHAPTER 46

Hiccup At The Office

Reaching the end of his bike ride, he was a bit winded and felt a tad out of shape. He leaned his bike against the gate and stretched. After cooling down, he felt really refreshed. He had an amazing ride and had seen some breathtaking sites. He had captured some gorgeous views on his camera. He felt full of energy and fulfilled. His mind was clear, and he was renewed from head to toe.

Clint finished tying down his bike and loaded the remaining part of his gear and reluctantly climbed into his Jeep. As he started the engine, he heard his phone ding. Nothing like the ding of a text message to bring you back down to earth. He unlocked his console and pulled out his phone. He had several missed calls and a couple text messages marked urgent. The first one read,

CALL THE OFFICE ASAP.

The second read,

CLINT, CALL ME! ASAP!

He dialed the office number, and the phone was answered immediately by an unfamiliar voice. It was male first of all. It was abrupt, "Law Office," the man answered. This was not the approved greeting.

"Who is this?" Clint asked.

"Who is this?" the man asked.

"This is Clint Winstead, I believe that you are in my law office. Where is my secretary?" he demanded with a sharp tone.

"Sir, you will need to report to your office by 6 p.m. this evening. We understand that you are away," the man stated as a matter of fact.

"Sir, with all due respect. Who am I speaking with and where is Merritt?" Clint asked firmly.

"Sir, with all due respect, your secretary is in the conference room with one of our agents," the man said.

"Agents?" Clint said with a raise in his voice. "What is going on?" he asked.

"Sir, my name is Franklin Carmichael, you may call me Mr. Carmichael. I am with the Federal Bureau of Investigation. At this time, I am requesting your presence by 6 p.m. this evening," the man said.

"Um...Mr. Carmichael sir...I am in the Wisconsin Dells. There is no way I will be able to make it to the office by 6 pm. What is this in regard to?" Clint asked.

"I am not at liberty to discuss this matter over the telephone. I suggest you come directly to the office as soon as you get in town. I will personally wait," the man said. Clint could tell this guy was in no mood for his sarcasm that was quickly building as a result of confusion and anger.

Clint did not like being in the unknown and this had him shaken to the core. "Sir, I will be there as soon as possible. Are you certain there isn't anything I can assist with over the telephone?" he asked.

"As I said before, I will not discuss any matters over the telephone. You must come directly to the office, or I will be forced to place a BOLO," the man said. Clint hated that kind of talk. He hated individuals who enjoyed the fact that they had authority over him.

He turned on the Jeep. He sat staring for what seemed like hours. What in the world had he gotten himself in to this time? This was not the first time that he had been questioned by the 'big dogs' as he called them. He always seemed to have an inside scoop that made him overly confident in dealing with this type. This time he was completely in the dark, or was he?

CHAPTER 47

Sister Talk With A Chance Of Tears

Tanner and Lexi headed toward the dock. The day was breezy and warm. It was a perfect September morning. They had packed a light blanket, some beer, a couple of sandwiches, and plenty of snacks to keep them fed through the day. They practically raced to the shed to retrieve the kayaks. Tanner's was red and Lexi had picked out a bright yellow one. The blue one belonged to their dad, and their mother did not have one. Although, they had a spare one that was green. The girls chose their boats and set them at the edge of the water. They barely exchanged two words as they were preparing for their short adventure to the island.

After each girl settled into their kayak, they slowly began paddling. Staying side by side, they began their sisterly chit-chat. "So, what have I missed?" Lexi started. "I talked to Sara; she said I should google some stuff that came out in the Tribune. You know what, knowing my case is over, I feel like a piece of the world has been lifted from my shoulders. Honestly, I don't care what happens at this point. I really want to focus on our day and our time together. I want to focus on what matters. I am getting married soon, and I just want to slow time down a bit and cherish all things that I hold dear," Tanner said.

"You know that just because you are getting married, doesn't mean that your past goes away," Lexi said. "I know, but things will change a bit," Tanner said. "Maybe some things, but not when it comes to me and you, NEVER!" Lexi said. "It has been amazing! I would not trade it for the world. We really had it good, and I thank God for it every day," Tanner added. "Me too!" Lexi agreed.

The girls made their way to the island, pulled their kayaks to the shore, and made their pallets for the day. For a while they both just laid staring at the clouds rolling by and the shapes that they were forming. It didn't take long before the old contest began. How many animals could be seen in a day and no duplicates. They chuckled. This game took them way back in time.

As the clouds became fewer and farther between, the girls grew hungry. They spread out the meal that they had prepared and spent the rest of the day sharing memories. As they came back around to the subject of Clint and Brint, the girls had covered every chapter it seemed from the third grade to the present. However, the Clint chapter stood out. "T, tell me about Clint? I mean, I know enough that I don't like him. But I know you, and I know your heart...there had to be good. You really loved him. I don't want to stir up anything bad, I am just curious," Lexi asked a trying request to her sister. Tanner took in a big breath of air and let out a sigh. "It's OK. I probably need to get it all out before I begin my forever," she said, and it was obvious that her tone had changed a bit. Pausing for a moment, as she collected her thoughts.

"So, when we were young, he used to tease me to the point that he was a complete jerk. I could not stand him. I did all I could to avoid him. He would seek me out at every function," Tanner explained. Pausing a moment before she began, "Do you remember the day mom and I were selling flowers and he came up to buy some and then turned around and gave them to me?" she asked Lexi. "I think so, I didn't pay much attention those days. I hated all of the events I was drug to. You know that's just not me," she said. "Well, we were going into our senior year of high school. We took a walk that day, and we talked about all of the years before and how he treated me...he says it was because he had a crush," Tanner said. "Why do guys do stuff like that? I mean the whole, if they are mean, they like you think," Lexi asked her to understand why. "I wish I knew, but what I found is that's only true when they are young. So that's where it began. When we went back to school, he called me every night. We would meet and go to the movies from time to time and it just grew slowly. That is what I think made it so sweet. He was always so considerate; he was a true gentleman. I remember our first kiss. He looked at me and asked if he could?" Tanner said smiling as she slowly picked apart her sandwich looking up to Lexi.

"Are you kidding?" Lexi said in disbelief. "No!" Tanner said in a convincing tone. "You know I don't go out on dates with guys. They are always friends, and we hang out," Lexi added. "Well, don't rush it, believe me it's not worth it," Tanner said. "That's what mom says! Back to the kiss," Lexi asked. "It was so sweet, I closed my eyes, and it seems like it took forever for our lips to touch…but when they did, they were like cotton candy. It felt like they melted with mine. I remember how my heart skipped a beat and my body felt warm from head to toe. It was gentle. It was kind. When he pulled away, he stared in my eyes, and I swear he was looking into my soul. We didn't talk for a bit after. It was like we were both trying to take it in. Then we just sat there staring out into the darkness. I think we were both trying to absorb the moment. I could not stop thinking about it for days. I had kissed guys before that I have kissed guys since, and I have never found one that had so much chemistry behind it," Tanner said blushing, as she looked out to the lake.

"Do you have that with Brint?" Lexi asked without hesitation. "No, it's better!" Tanner said as a smile suddenly was beaming across her face. "How?" Lexi asked. "See, he and I have everything, not just the chemistry.

The first time I kissed Brint, it was amazing, but it didn't make me tingle. What it did have was a promise of depth. It made me feel safe. It had substance. When I look back on my relationship with Clint, we had a lot of fun, and we made some awesome memories. We definitely had the chemistry, but we didn't have the rest of the pieces. What pieces exactly, I couldn't tell you, but there were pieces missing. What is scary is that I didn't know pieces were missing at the time. When I am with Brint, it is like I have everything. Please don't ask me to describe everything. It is just something you know is there," she said.

"What happened with Clint? Like what made dad so upset? I remember that night that he was ready to get in the car and go to him," Lexi asked. "I think dad really thought that Clint would become part of the family. Then, when he turned into a complete jerk, he was disappointed, and I think he was hurt a little too," Tanner said sighing. "He treated you terribly, didn't he?" Lexi asked. "It was gut wrenching. I will never forget going to his house after a game, and it was obvious his friends were trying to keep me busy and occupied. Later I found out he had taken another girl to the game, and she was leaving as I was arriving. I learned after the fact that he would take me to lunch and take many others out to dinner when I would be studying. Every time I tried to break things off, he would turn on the charm and I would be right back in his arms. He knew exactly what to say.

College really turned him into a heartless piece of work," Tanner explained. "You know I have never had a broken heart," Lexi admitted. "And I hope you never do. It's the worst pain I have ever experienced. However, I am so thankful that I went through it. I am a stronger, better person for having gone down that road. Actually, I am so glad that I went down the many broken roads I did. I feel like I have lived. I have felt ultimate joy and ultimate pain. It brought me closer to my Savior and definitely strengthened our relationship. I tell you, there were some days, nights, no, hours that I seriously did not think I would make it through, and God carried me. He gave me strength to find my self-worth. So, with that pain came the greatest gift, and I wouldn't trade it for the world," Tanner explained smiling and looking up to the sky.

"I admire you for always looking for the good in the midst of ugly. You have always done that," Lexi said. "So, I am glad he has found a fresh start. I think what hurt so badly is I know, and knew, the person that he could be, and I could always see the potential. I kept believing in that. I am so glad I went through that heartbreak. It gave me clarity on what I wanted and what I was not willing to settle for. Brint is my guy. He is my forever, and I have no doubts. Looking back, I would go through it all again to be the person that I am today," Tanner said as she wiped a tear from her right eye...she did not want Lexi to see it.

"I hope I find my Brint one day. So far, no luck." Dad said I'll kick them to the curb before I give them a chance. "I told him that I don't put up with any nonsense," Lexi said sniggering. "Good for you Lexi! Don't ever put yourself in a position like I did. It was mental abuse; it was physical abuse and Brint has never made me feel less of a person in any way. God led me through a very broken path to get to him. I think I had to go through that to appreciate him. I am so thankful, Lexi," Tanner added. A tear ran down Tanner's face. Lexi reached over to wipe it away.

God carried me. He gave me strength to find my self-worth. So, with that pain came the greatest gift, and I wouldn't trade it for the world," Tanner explained smiling and looking up to the sky.

"I admire you for always looking for the good in the midst of ugly. You have always done that," Lexi said. "So, I am glad he has found a fresh start. I think what hurt so badly is I know, and knew, the person that he could be, and I could always see the potential. I kept believing in that. I am so glad I went through that heartbreak. It gave me clarity on what I wanted and what I was not willing to settle for. Brint is my guy. He is my forever, and I have no doubts. Looking back, I would go through it all again to be the person that

I am today," Tanner said as she wiped a tear from her right eye...she did not want Lexi to see it.

"I hope I find my Brint one day. So far, no luck." Dad said I'll kick them to the curb before I give them a chance. "I told him that I don't put up with any nonsense," Lexi said sniggering. "Good for you Lexi! Don't ever put yourself in a position like I did. It was mental abuse; it was physical abuse and Brint has never made me feel less of a person in any way. God led me through a very broken path to get to him. I think I had to go through that to appreciate him. I am so thankful, Lexi," Tanner added. A tear ran down Tanner's face. Lexi reached over to wipe it away.

"Why are you crying?" she asked. "Because I feel so much love that I cannot put it in to words." Brint always says, "Your feelings are running down your face again," Tanner said as she thought of how he would wipe her tears away. "That's sweet!" Lexi said. "You know I cry when I am frustrated, mad, happy, in love," she said. "Yep!" Lexi agreed. "See, Clint saw it as being weak. Brint says it is a sign of strength," Tanner said. "I see. I really see," Lexi said and hugged her sister as they laid back on her blanket. Staring at the setting sun, she prayed silently. Tanner wiped her face and laid back just the same and praised God for the many roads she had traveled to bring her to her current life.

CHAPTER 48

Clint's Cuffing

Clint didn't bother to turn on the radio as he headed toward the office. If he concentrated really hard, he could focus on the roar of the tires against the asphalt. Mostly all he could hear were the many voices in his head. He wanted to call his father to converse with him. He chose not to, because his dad would try to fix it, and this was his mess. His dad had warned him many times to be careful when dealing with the Copelands. They had a way of reeling you in deep.

As the conversations and meetings replayed in his mind, he remembered the trip to the Cayman Islands where he and Sr. Copeland had met with a couple of "financiers" as Cope had called them. They were wined and dined to the max. Clint remembered it felt like he was royalty for the week. They talked millions that would turn into billions if all went as planned. Clint didn't follow much of the conversation as there were many aspects that had already been in play for a while it seemed.

He never thought to debrief with his father. All he remembered were the hours he spent at the bank and on the phone setting up eleven different accounts as requested. His firm assisted in the purchase and sale of several large plots of land, and he knew the money was flowing heavily. It all appeared simple and above board. He tried to remember details, but the closer he got to his exit the more jumbled his thoughts became. His hands became sweaty, and he felt like he couldn't breathe.

As he walked in the office, he saw Merritt sitting in the conference room. She looked stiff. She was wiping her face with a handkerchief; he assumed one of the men in suits had given her. Merritt glanced up at him as he appeared in the hallway. He felt the blood run out of his face when he saw her poised in her chair, one leg crossed behind the other, papers scattered in front of her. One man was standing behind her looking over her shoulder. The other man was seated to her left. His back was turned as he was facing her. He was pounding his finger on the table while pointing at something. Merritt just kept shaking her head back and forth. He could hear a voice raise slightly.

Once the man that was standing behind Merritt noticed my presence, he nodded in my direction and excused himself from his post. Opening the door, he wasted no time. "Clint Winstead!" the man shouted. "Yes!" Clint answered. "Follow me!" the man said abruptly and headed in the direction of the library. As Clint passed his office, he noticed all the file cabinet drawers were open and there were individuals pulling files. Another man was at his desk hooked to the computer.

"Sir, as you can see, we are executing on a search warrant served on your firm today," the man said. "Can you tell me what grounds you have for this?" Clint demanded. "Have a seat," the man said as he lowered his voice to normal tone. "No, I think I will stand thank you," Clint said firmly as he folded his arms. "We have a warrant for your arrest on the grounds of multiple accounts of bank fraud and money laundering," the man explained. "Excuse me?" Clint said in disbelief. "Sir, there will be plenty of time for questions, place your hands behind your back," the man commanded as he handcuffed Clint.

The gentleman immediately began reading him his rights as he strongly encouraged him physically back toward the elevator doors. Once they were downstairs, the elevator doors opened, a black Chevrolet Tahoe met them. There were flashing lights from the photographers who had gathered, and he assumed they had been alerted that he had arrived. He never made eye contact.

CHAPTER 49
Tanner's Prayer

When Tanner and Lexi returned to the house, they noticed their dad's white 1961 Mercedes-Benz 190 SL parked in the driveway. "T, look mom and dad are here...or at least dad," Lexi said. "I don't remember him telling me they were coming by," Tanner said. The girls quickly pulled their kayaks from the water and carried them to the shed. They were taught to always put "it" away where you found it. Take care of your stuff, and you will have it forever was the gist of the teaching. As was the case with her dad's Benz. It had been her grandfather's, and when he passed away, their dad was gifted the car. It was his pride and joy.

The girls ran up the steps and saw their mom sitting by the gas fire pit, which was pleasant to look at and was relaxing but didn't come close to competing with the massive stone fire pit. The smell of burning wood always touched Tanner's soul. She found it comforting. "Mom!" Tanner yelled approaching the top step. Her mother rose from her seated position and almost ran to the screened door. "My girls! How precious it was to see you two coming across the cove. It brought back so many memories. Did you enjoy your day?" she asked. The excitement in their mother's voice was almost childlike. "We did. It was one of the best!" Tanner said.

"They're back!" Madeline shouted.

As they all walked into the living room, their dad was seated in his recliner chair, mixed drink in hand. The nightly news was cranked up. Spencer lowered the footrest and rose. He held his arms open wide, and both girls practically ran toward the offered embrace. Spencer held his girls as tight as he could. They were his world. Madeline joined them. From within the pile, Lexi yelled, "Group hug!" It was their special moment. This was one of the most special memories Tanner would keep close for as long as she lived. All of them together, one family for the last time. For the next time they were all together in a 'group hug,' there would be one more in the pile. Brint. She smiled just thinking how wonderful it would be.

The next few days flew by. Tanner could barely remember each day as she laid down each night. Her days were filled from the moment she opened her eyes with wrapping up all of the loose ends for her perfect day. Tonight, as she laid down, she felt super peaceful. She knew with all of her heart that she was exactly where she was supposed to be.

The crickets were loud in their chorus presentation tonight, but that didn't distract Tanner from her thoughts. She was feeling very thankful this particular evening and decided to get out of bed and kneel beside her bed. She folded her hands in front of her and gently rested her elbows on the bed. She leaned her forehead against her folded hands, closed her eyes and let out a whisper.

"Dear Father in heaven, You are all knowing. I have come to You in times of struggle, despair, grief, and heartache. I have come to You in admiration and thankfulness. I have come to You in ultimate wonder and question. You have been forever faithful. I am thankful to have moments in my life where I could physically see and experience grace and mercy. I can see evidence of Your answered prayers. I can see evidence where You did not answer prayers, and, for that. I am grateful. I know the plans You have laid for me, and I am so thankful for Your guidance. I am thankful for Your faithfulness, when I wasn't willing or when I didn't choose to see Your works of Your plan. You never left me when I left You. Tonight, I come to You in prayer. Again, I am asking for Your blessing on my life. I want You to be the center of my life, my marriage and will give You my word that I will do my best to honor You with my marriage journey. I am forever thankful for the many blessings and for the one that You brought to me in Brint. I know we are not a perfect people, but we were made for one another. With all I have, thank You," she prayed.

As her prayer came to an end, she climbed beneath the sheets and snuggled into place. The chaos from the previous weeks and days seemed far, far away. She was at complete peace, because she believed with all of her heart that she had endured her journey. She also knew that it was just beginning.

CHAPTER 50

Day Of Reckoning

As he was placed in the back of the Tahoe, he sat staring at the floor. The carpet was black. The longer he stared, the more entranced he became, like looking into a deep dark hole that had no end in sight. He kept thinking that this was indicative of the mess he had created. He couldn't stop thinking about the two accounts he had set up for Copeland and their recent requests to liquidate land in a hurry. He also thought about the many vehicles that Copeland had paid him with including the Mercedes AMG. The Jeep was old and was purchased with money that he had made while he was in college. It was legally his.

He started thinking about the building he lived in and how he was given such a discount to live on the top floor of the condo complex that Copeland owned. He thought about the "business trips" that his family went on when he was growing up. The Copeland family had been represented by Clint's family for as long as he could remember. The beach house in the Keys. He began to realize his whole life had been funded by dirty money.

Had he been a part of a money laundering scheme and not known it? Worse, had his dad known and not thought to tell him? Had he not been listening to his father? He began scrolling through the many conversations

in his mind and realized, no, his dad had done things right. He and Senior Copeland had gone way back. It wasn't until his father had turned all business over to him that things changed. His dad had played it strait while he was willing to compromise his character for the big gains.

He was disappointed in himself. Suddenly an overwhelming feeling came over him. Thinking to himself, yes, my father will be terribly disappointed in me, but more important, my heavenly Father. Breaking the silence, "Oh, what have I done? Father in heaven, what have I done? My ego has been fed by corruption and need to feel powerful. I have lost the only girl I ever loved and now my life."

Clint continued to stare at the blackness when he felt the truck coming to a stop. He looked up for a moment to see more reporters as they made their turn in to what was the underground garage of the jail. He took in a deep breath. Suddenly, he felt in his heart that he was not alone. He knew he would be forgiven. However, he also knew without a shadow of a doubt, that from this point forward, he would need to do life the right way. He immediately began by dropping his pompous attitude as the car door opened and made his way into the jail.

CHAPTER 51

Happily Ever After

Brint and his family arrived in Norris the following Thursday afternoon. He couldn't wait to see Tanner. They were greeted by her family at the door. Her aunts, uncles, and cousins had also arrived. It was a warm gathering. Everyone was sharing stories and laughing. He could not remember a time when complete strangers had made him feel so loved. He knew he was exactly where he was supposed to be...with Tanner at his side for life.

About the Author

KELLY RAE WHITED

Kelly grew up in Pigeon Forge, Tennessee, and resides in Corryton, TN, about five miles outside of Knoxville. She spends her days as a personal banker, although she considers her most important job is being a mother to her eleven-year-old, daughter, Carleigh. She and her husband, Scott of sixteen years, enjoy spending time camping with Carleigh and Myranda, her stepdaughter. Myranda is married with three children.

Growing up at the foot of the Great Smoky Mountains National Park has given Kelly the appreciation of all things created by God. She loves enjoying the fresh air on a short hike. She also enjoys boating on the lake. As a young girl, her parents had a houseboat on Norris Lake, where she has many fond memories. As an adult, she has spent many hours on Norris with her family, and it is also where she met her husband.

Kelly wrote her first short story the summer of 1990. Since then, she went on to receive a Bachelor of Science in Business and Organizational Management from Tusculum College in Greenville, TN. Determined to fulfill her dreams of becoming a writer, she finished her first book in the fall of 2020.

The Right Way: Crossroads of Fresh Starts, debuts as her first book, but it won't be her last. Kelly draws upon her own life experience and feelings to create a storyline. She hopes her readers will be able to relate to and create a glimpse of hope. If Kelly could share a universal message; it would be that we could all be a bit more forgiving of our own short comings and those of others, allowing us to treat others with respect and love.